SUPERIOR
DECEPTION

Other books by Matthew Williams:

Superior Death

SUPERIOR DECEPTION

•

Matthew Williams

AVALON BOOKS
NEW YORK

Published by Thomas Bouregy & Co., Inc.
160 Madison Avenue, New York, NY 10016

Library of Congress Cataloging-in-Publication Data

Williams, Matthew, 1963–
  Superior deception / Matthew Williams.
    p. cm.
  ISBN 978-0-8034-9869-3 (acid-free paper)
  1. Reporters and reporting—Fiction. 2. Michigan—Fiction.
I. Title.

  PS3623.I55868S873 2007
  813'.6—dc22

                                        2007024710

PRINTED IN THE UNITED STATES OF AMERICA
ON ACID-FREE PAPER
BY HADDON CRAFTSMEN, BLOOMSBURG, PENNSYLVANIA

This book is dedicated to Suzanne.
Her suggestions made it a better story,
and her encouragement made it possible.
This is also dedicated to Sam, a talented
writer and illustrator in his own right.

I'd like to thank Detective Captain L. "Mike" Angeli with the Marquette City Police Department for sharing his knowledge and coffee, and the women of the "Between the Sheets" Book Club for teaching me attention to detail.

Chapter One

How do you explain to your toddler that the man dangling from a noose isn't playing on a rope swing?

I probably didn't handle it the best way. Then again, I didn't expect to find a well-respected community philanthropist hanging from an ancient maple in Explorer's Park during our father-daughter outing.

Five minutes earlier we'd been rocking on spring-loaded animals and watching the Manitou River ripple past. Fog rising off the water's tea-colored surface hid the far bank and made it seem as if the golden birch leaves, the first to change each September, were glowing.

Until the "William Tell Overture" sounded from my pocket, the only things we'd heard were an occasional gull's cry, the plaintive sigh of our harbor's foghorn, and, of course, my daughter's babble.

Glory took off running when she heard the ring tone assigned to Lou Kendricks, editor and owner of the *Apostle Bay Chronicle*. My boss is an old-school journalist from

Chicago who bought the *Chronicle* at auction and is spending his retirement—and his second chance at life—rebuilding our beleaguered paper. He doesn't understand the concept of days off.

Between his demands and my own lame attempts to wean myself from the police scanner and my cell phone, I've been dragging Glory to work on days I'm supposed to be playing tea party and reading Dr. Seuss. My daughter's learned to compete for my attention at these times by engaging in life-threatening activities.

Knowing that, I lunged off the fiberglass frog, hoping to snag a handful of pink hoodie. No such luck.

"What's up, Lou?" I said.

Ahead, Glory turned left past a big cedar and headed down the riverbank. I shouted for her to stop, but that's about the same as cheering her onward.

"Get your tail in here," he growled, most likely holding the phone against one droopy jowl with a shoulder while his perpetually bloodshot eyes scanned the wire and his meaty paws pounded his keyboard. The guy has the looks and tenacity of a hound.

"We're in it up to our eyeballs this morning," he said.

I knew why too. Last night's heated city council meeting and the protest outside city hall would undoubtedly be filling page one. And since our local television station devoted several minutes of airtime to the story, including video of my wife Deb, leading the protesters, Lou no doubt wanted a fresh angle this morning.

That meant he'd want me handling the extraneous stuff: briefs, the vessel report, and probably some page layout, while he and our city beat reporter, Mort Maki, drummed up something new.

Deb and friends were protesting the planned development of Explorer's Park and its mile or so of Lake Superior shore line. We live in a harbor town on the southern shore of the big lake, close enough to the North Pole that we have to drive south to visit Toronto. And depending on whom you talk to, we're either about to enter the greatest era of economic prosperity since our founder, Randolph Sorenson, built his first boat pier, or we're heading down a path of urban and environmental destruction that must be stopped at all cost.

Sorenson's heirs gave Explorer's Park to the city to be protected for future generations. That gift included about a mile of sand beach—split in half by the Manitou River—and a memorial garden honoring the Apostles, the twelve explorers who landed here in the 1840s.

Our current mayor, Jack Reynolds, has interpreted—Deb would say *twisted*—the Sorenson family's proviso to mean the property should be developed into condos, hotels, a boardwalk, and restaurants. The mayor's argument—successful, considering that the council approved his plan last night—is that we'll benefit far more from economic development than from a land use that doesn't generate revenue. And he likes to add that Sorenson, the entrepreneur who built this city, would certainly agree—even though Sorenson's current heir doesn't.

That's part of the reason I brought Glory here this morning. Besides the fact that I've had enough of *Teletubbies* to last a lifetime, I wanted to enjoy the park's trails and playground before they're gone.

But as I rounded the cedar, caught sight of my daughter at the river's edge, looking over her shoulder to see if I was chasing her, I couldn't help thinking this wasn't exactly the morning I'd planned.

I skidded down an incline layered with moist pine needles,

only half listening to Lou's litany, and chased Glory along a fisherman's path. Dew soaked my shoes and pants.

Relieved when she turned away from the river and ran, giggling, up the bank toward higher ground, I reined in my breathing and interrupted Lou. "It's my day off, remember? And I've got Glory."

"Get your wife or mother to take her for a while," he said.

"Deb's working. Why can't Ashley handle it? That's why you hired her—to fill the gap when I'm out."

I lost sight of Glory and scanned the park. Ahead was a deserted picnic area, its pavilion a shadow in the fog. To my left I caught a glimpse of pink bobbing between cedar branches toward the arched timber bridge that crosses the Manitou.

"Ashley's AWOL," Lou said.

I took off running and hit the bridge's planks as Glory exited the far side. She cast a glance back when she reached the semicircle of lilacs that are part of the Apostle Memorial. Assured I was following, she squeezed through the bushes.

Lou yelled something about not caring if Maki had to wake the man. Then he added, "Vince, if you don't get in here, our deadline's toast."

I circled the lilacs to an opening and jumped forward, hoping to nab the little buckaroo. Instead, a white flash blinded me.

Blinking away the red spots before my eyes and reaching for my daughter, I said, "Lou, I found your missing reporter. And, um . . . you can forget about that deadline."

Chapter Two

Short both in size and manners, Ashley Adams doesn't waste words on social niceties. She doesn't believe in gray areas. She is always right. Indeed, Ashley's pretty much the way I was at her age. She's five months out of the Michigan State School of Journalism and in a hurry to win the Pulitzer—unlikely at a small-time paper like the *Chronicle,* so I'm not sure why she came to Apostle Bay several weeks ago.

Theoretically I'm her mentor, training her to cover my former beats while I settle into my part-time role writing features and helping Lou with special sections.

Ashley's made it clear she has no interest in my advice.

"You're in the picture," she said, neither lowering the camera nor waiting for me to move before shooting again. I lifted Glory to one hip and turned her head away from the gruesome scene and the camera.

My first hope when I saw the body swinging from the ancient maple, considering the mist, autumn chill, and changing leaves, was that Ashley had staged a Halloween photo.

But I recognized the man's salt-and-pepper goatee, despite the odd way the noose forced down his head. Suspended maybe an arm's length from us, draped in black judicial robes, his black Mezlan shoes inches above the wood chips, hung Judge Dexter Sorenson.

"That's the judge," I said. I held Glory's head averted despite her best efforts to see.

Ashley waved me to one side. "You're still in the frame."

Glory squirmed and kept saying "rope swing" in her little tyke's voice. Ashley snapped photos. Lou shouted through the phone I now held by my side.

I flipped it closed, knowing it might drive the man to the verge of his second heart attack but unable to deal with him at the moment. I carried Glory over to the granite memorial fifteen feet away, told her to stay put, then came back to Ashley.

"Have you called 9-1-1?"

She lowered the camera, gave me a look that implied I was an idiot, and then said, "I found him. It's my story."

"You haven't called the cops?"

"He's already dead," she said, stepping closer to the body. "You do it while I get a few more photos."

I knew the judge—a noble man who played oboe in the symphony, who opened his home for the annual garden tour, who was reputed to wear a tie and pressed shirt even when cops arrived at his house at odd hours seeking his signature on a warrant. I know he would be mortified for people to remember him this way.

I flipped the phone open again but also followed Ashley toward the body, curiosity stronger than common sense. She reached out and turned Sorenson so his chest was toward us and nodded at a sheet of paper pinned to his robe. It curled away from his body, and I couldn't see more than a blur of color.

"Sick, isn't it?"

I thought she meant the dead man, but before I could stay her hand, she reached out and flattened the paper's edges. It was a nasty photo, the kind of porn you'd figure only creeps would find on the Internet. Beneath the picture, printed in shaky, block letters:

I CAN'T LIVE WITH MYSELF.

Ashley snapped a photo of it. "I doubt Lou has the guts to use it," she said.

Glory came from behind us and pushed the judge's body with her small hands, setting it swaying.

"Glory!" I lifted her away—too forcefully, I'm sure. "We've got to call the cops," I said, backing away, holding Glory tightly against my chest. "Something's not right here."

"Duh," Ashley said. "The sicko killed himself."

She popped open a side panel on the camera, took out the memory card, and pocketed it. Then she tossed the camera my way. I reached out and caught it before it hit the ground.

"*Ciao,* Vince. I have a deadline to make."

Chapter Three

Ashley moved fast. I was still gaping, holding the emptied camera and wondering why she'd left it with me, when she disappeared into the fog and trees, heading toward the parking lot. When I recovered and called after her, a snarling voice stopped me.

"Freeze, newsman."

I knew without looking that it was Detective Archie "Speed Demon" Freeman, the Dirty Harry wannabe of Apostle Bay and the only person to call me that stupid name. Freeman skidded past us on his police issue mountain bike, the mode of transportation he'd been relegated to—by Judge Sorenson, no less. He sprayed wood chips toward the body and, I noticed, reached for the sidearm he was no longer allowed to carry. Glory, for the first time that morning, seemed to understand that playtime was over.

I groaned. Why is it that every time I find myself in some compromising position, this joker appears? We'd met a year earlier, at the scene of another death, where he'd tried to confiscate my camera. I was saved that time by police chief Dale Weathers, who happens to be my godfather as well as Freeman's boss. My relationship with Freeman has been downhill since.

It's partly my fault. After a few initial attempts at civility I've been less than respectful to the detective. I took immense pleasure covering the legal debacle that earned him the nickname Speed Demon, which we used in a *Chronicle* headline after he drove his unmarked sedan onto thin ice while chasing two snowmobiles.

That sedan, his second wrecked vehicle of the year, now sits five fathoms down in our harbor and is a minor attraction to boaters and scuba divers. Freeman maintains that the sledders were driving with excessive speed and he was attempting to ticket them. They, on the other hand, took advantage of his overzealous reputation to claim they thought a maniac was chasing them, and they fled in fear for their lives.

The two victims—they and their vehicles plunged into icy waters—sued. Judge Sorenson heard the case. After viewing the video of the chase, salvaged from the dash-mounted camera in Freeman's submerged car, the judge gave the city two choices: A) ban Detective Freeman from motorized vehicle use for one year, and require him to wear a uniform while on duty; or B) cough up a pile of cash for property damages and pain and suffering.

The city council went for option A and with unusual forethought also told the chief to take away Freeman's weapon.

I think Speed Demon took the judge's ruling a little too personally, and that's why he's running what was, until this morning, a hopeless campaign against Sorenson for circuit court judge.

Freeman's slogan: *I'm tough enough to do some real damage to crime*. It would be more accurate without the last two words.

"It's Judge Sorenson," I said, nodding at the body. "He's dead."

Freeman stepped forward and snatched the camera from me. He demanded my cell phone.

"C'mon, detective, Glory and I were playing, and—"

"Do it!" he shouted.

I tossed him the phone and then pulled Glory, who was now trembling, more closely against my chest. She buried her face in my coat.

Freeman loosed the handcuffs from his belt.

"Put the cuffs away, Freeman."

"Stick a cork in it," he said. "You're a suspect." He grabbed my arm and snapped a cuff on me before I had a chance to move. Then he looked around for a place to anchor me and decided his rear bike wheel would have to suffice. He pulled me toward it, ordered me to sit, and locked me to the rear tire.

"Maybe you ought to—"

"If you know what's good for you, you'll shut up," he said.

I bit my tongue, knowing this was more payback for our past run-ins than anything else. I'd be better off saving it until the chief arrived.

I brushed Glory's hair with my fingers. She snuggled against me, something that didn't happen too often, and I told her that everything would be fine.

Freeman called dispatch, described the scene, then snapped on a pair of latex gloves from his saddlebag and examined the judge.

"Figures," I heard him mutter when he looked at the paper pinned to Sorenson's chest.

A small breeze came up, rattling the leaves and stirring the judge's robes. Sirens bayed in the distance.

"We'll be out of this soon, sweetheart," I whispered.

Chapter Four

When the chief arrived, he was less empathetic with our situation than I'd hoped. The sight of Glory, whom he treats like a grandchild, tempered his anger, but his tone and fierce gray eyes told me I was in for a lecture once she was gone.

"Your mom will be here in a few minutes to take Glory," he said.

"Thanks, Chief."

He held out a hand to my daughter. She climbed from my lap and took it, her toddler fingers disappearing in his mammoth grip.

"Hi, Chief," she said, as if they hung out together every day.

"Hi there, little Mornin' Glory."

He told Freeman to release me. The detective did so, glaring the entire time. When I was free, I followed the chief and Glory to his black sedan. He opened the rear door and told us to wait inside the vehicle.

"Chief, this isn't—"

"Save it," he growled. "This is not what I need this morning.

We've got our hands full with some nut job who hot-wired a backhoe and tore up the cemetery last night, the mayor's breathing down my neck about the protesters at city hall, and the council's threatening to slash my budget. This is not what I need," he repeated as he walked away.

I propped Glory on my lap, and we watched through the open door, Glory fascinated by the flashing lights and activity. The morning walkers—retired folks and parents with babies in jogging strollers—were filtering into the park now, gawking at the scene. The chief sent Freeman to head them off with a roll of yellow tape.

Detective Captain Gordon Greenleaf arrived next, driving his white, unmarked sedan on the wood-chip path. An ambulance from St. Luke's Hospital followed him, as well as a sheriff's deputy, either stopping by to see if the city cops needed help or, more likely, to catch a glimpse of the corpse.

Gordon, a head taller than everyone else, inspected the judge, then consulted with the chief. They spoke a few moments, Gord glancing once our way, then Gord took off. The chief told the EMTs to cool their heels, and then he sent the deputy to help Freeman with the small crowd of onlookers.

Either the first people here had been calling friends, or a larger than usual crowd was arriving at the park, like me, because of last night's council decision. I heard Freeman's voice rising and saw he was clearing a path for the blue van from the state police crime lab.

Glory fidgeted and bounced on the chief's rear seat. I should have been distracting her in some way, but I couldn't keep my eyes off the whole strange scene. Seeing Mom arrive was a relief. The chief waved her over, said a few things to the crime scene techs as they unloaded gear, and then guided her to us.

"Hi, Mom," I said.

Glory leaped out of the sedan at her. "Nana!" she cried.

An athletic woman who spends most of her time outdoors, Mom had no trouble catching my daughter and swinging her up into a bear hug. The way her Norwegian eyes light up whenever she's with Glory is gratifying. She gave me a little squeeze too, something she'd have been afraid to do last year.

"I can't believe it's Judge Sorenson," she said over Glory's shoulder.

"I know," I said, thinking there'd be plenty of shocked folks when today's *Chronicle* hit the street.

"This is no place for a little girl," the chief said.

"Sure, I get the message," Mom replied. "You want us out of here. How long will you be, Vince? I've got my bridge group at one but would be glad to back out for an extra afternoon with Glory."

"That's up to the chief," I said, shrugging my shoulders. "Speed Demon said I'm a suspect—of what, I'm not sure."

"What—" my mother started. She turned toward the chief, who was glowering at me. "I thought you were just keeping him—"

"We need to ask Vince a few questions," the chief interrupted. "That's all. He'll be along in an hour or so."

Then the chief stepped closer to my mother and mumbled something I couldn't hear. She nodded and carried Glory away. My daughter looked back over her shoulder and waved.

The chief waited until they were out of earshot and then turned on me. "If you'd learn to keep your smart comments to yourself, you wouldn't be in this fix."

"That's not fair, Chief. I was just—"

"Detective Freeman followed correct procedure. You were

discovered with a dead man, at a possible crime scene, tampering with evidence—"

"Wha—"

"You should be glad that you've been treated so well."

"Cuffed to a bike tire and threatened while playing in the park with my daughter?"

"Come off it, Vince," the chief said, disappointment on his face. "Sure, you probably came here with Glory, but when you discovered the judge, you started taking photos for the *Chronicle* instead of calling 9-1-1 as you should have. I expect better from you."

"So that's what Mom meant," I said, figuring out why the chief had detained me. "You think you're keeping this out of today's newspaper. Guess what? If either you or Freeman had spent less time telling me to shut up, you'd have learned that it's already on the front page, photos and story."

"Excuse me?" the chief said.

"Yeah, what I tried to tell you and your hotshot detective is that Glory and I weren't the first ones here this morning. That would be Ashley Adams."

"That new girl?"

"Girl? C'mon, Chief, you're dating yourself."

"But you had the—"

I smiled. "Aren't you the one who's always telling me not to assume things? I had Ashley's camera, but she has the memory card with the photos. She popped it out, tossed me the camera, and took off moments before Freeman—excuse me, *Detective* Freeman—arrived. It was either incredibly good luck that she disappeared exactly when she did, or she saw him coming and booked out of here, leaving me holding the bag. Pretty clever on her part, don't you think?"

The chief ran a hand over his silver brush cut, a sure sign he was trying to contain his rage.

"But . . . what was she doing here?"

"Considering she was supposed to be at city hall checking the morning dispatch log? I think that's an interesting question."

Chapter Five

After the chief cut me loose, I drove to the office, parked behind the building, and then slipped between the rural route carriers crowded around the *Chronicle*'s rear entrance. Inside, I passed the giant rollers thumping out another day's version of local news and nodded at the press foreman, who was inspecting a copy for quality. I held my breath against the ink and solvent odors and passed the inserters, who were stuffing ads into the papers as they rolled off the press and down a wheeled ramp.

I grabbed a copy and checked Ashley's photo. It covered the top right quadrant of the page, where it would be the first thing seen on newsstands throughout Apostle Bay and the surrounding county. I was relieved Lou didn't use one with Glory and me in the background.

Upstairs in an open bull pen of desks and computers, I found Lou Kendricks holding court at his workstation in the room's center. Our editorial staff surrounded him for the daily, post-deadline planning session.

Lou ignored me as I grabbed a chair and sat on the periphery while he finished with the sports guy and with Gina Holt, our paper's longtime editorial clerk, office manager, obit writer, sometime gossip columnist, and lead cynic. Gina, her voice scratchy from a lifetime of smoking, is the only staff member Lou can't stare down.

Our other news reporter, Mort Maki, gaunt despite continuous junk food consumption, sat hunched over his desk nursing a Fanta orange pop.

Ashley sat across from him, tapping on her PDA. I wantcd to glare at her for ditching me this morning, but she ignored me. I gave up after a moment and scanned her story about the judge, almost choking when I read her lead.

APOSTLE BAY-Judge Dexter Sorenson was found dead this morning, hanged by a noose from a tree in Explorer's Park, an apparent suicide that mimics another well-known suicide some 150 years earlier at the same site, possibly the same tree.

Another well-known suicide? I'd never heard that. How could Ashley, such a recent transplant here, have possibly dug up that fact on deadline?

I read on, impressed, downright envious to find that she'd not only unearthed that historic tidbit, but she'd also landed a quote from the judge's nephew, who'd been living in Apostle Bay with the judge since early summer. Peter Sorenson, according to her story, was the judge's sole heir.

I finished the story and decided that she'd overplayed the porn photo and suicide angle, but it would certainly get the town humming with gossip and sell a lot of newsstand copies.

I flipped back from the jump page to reread her opening,

but before I had the chance, Lou dismissed the sports guy and jumped down my throat.

"The two biggest stories to hit this town in your lifetime, and you come strolling in after the press is already rolling," he said. He jabbed a gnawed pencil toward me and added, "I don't think this arrangement where you pick your own hours is working."

"Wait a minute," I protested. "I'm not even supposed to be here today, and thanks to Ashley I've been—"

"Thanks to Ashley, we have an outstanding story—with art."

I glanced at her. She continued tapping on her PDA, but I saw the smirk.

"Yeah, I've been wondering about that," I said, still watching her. "Weren't you supposed to be at city hall this morning?"

She looked up and met my gaze. "Jealous?"

"Knock it off," Lou interrupted. "We need a plan for tomorrow."

"No, I'm not jealous," I said, lying. "Just curious how you happened to—"

"I said, knock it off!"

The room went silent.

Then Maki belched.

"Whoops," he said.

Ashley went back to tapping her PDA.

Now that Lou had our attention, he continued, "Here's what I want for tomorrow: Ashley, follow up on the judge's death. Find out what the cops have to say. Will they confirm it's a suicide? And I want more on this porn angle. See if they find anything in his home or office that backs up what you saw today."

"I'd be careful—" I started.

"Let me worry about that," Lou cut me off. "Also, Ashley, get with the photog. I want pics of Sorenson's house and his chambers. Write a sidebar on the judge's most public cases, his impact on the court, et cetera. Vince will help you on background."

"I can handle it myself," she said.

"No, you can't," Lou countered. "You're going to have your hands full, and Vince has covered the judge the last few years. He can save you the legwork."

Lou paused and sipped from one of the three mugs on his desk. He always had several in various states of freshness, but you could never tell from his expression if he'd sipped the correct one.

He nodded at me. "Draft a history of the judge's tenure, and get it to her by this evening. Also, I want you to write a sidebar on Sorenson's philanthropy, what it's meant to the community. See if you can find out whether it will continue after his death. The nephew seems willing to talk. Pin him down on details."

"I'll take that," Ashley said.

"No, you've got enough on your plate."

"But Peter, the nephew—he's *my* contact," she said. "I'll cover it."

"The guy's a total dork," Maki piped in. "Showed up at the meeting last night dressed in a hunting jacket that was right off the cover of an Orvis catalog. I heard him moaning about our being such a hick town 'cause we don't even have a Starbucks. Can you believe that?"

"Do you have a number for him?" I asked.

"I said I'll handle it," Ashley snapped. "I've got to talk with him anyway to arrange the photos, so it makes sense."

I expected Lou to argue, but I noticed he was smiling and nodding his head.

"Good thinking," he said. "You handle the philanthropy angle too. Vince, instead, we'll need a small piece for tomorrow about what's going to happen at the court. Who'll hear Sorenson's cases? Who appoints a replacement? Will someone be appointed with the election only two months away? You know the drill. Of course, only if you can fit it into your schedule."

I held my tongue, not trusting myself to say anything wise. Lou and I needed to have a chat after the meeting.

"Good," he said. "TV will be all over this stuff tonight. The AP's sending in their Northern Michigan guy, and we might even see someone from the Freep," he said, referring to the *Detroit Free Press*. "I want to make sure we're running in the lead with this. Got it? Because if you don't, you can move up front to classifieds and spend your mornings rewriting ad copy."

I nodded, thinking we were probably catching a glimpse of the old Lou from his time at the *Chicago Herald*, the time before a heart attack sent him into temporary retirement and he'd moved up here to die.

"Mort, I want you on the Explorer's Park development angle. The judge was a vocal opponent of the shoreline project. Is this going to change anything with the council? Will it delay the project? Get reaction from the protesters and also from Jack Reynolds. Make sure you and Ashley touch base if either of you find a connection between his death and the development.

"Also, Mort, you've got to flesh out today's story. It wasn't quite up to par with our other page-one piece. Get more details about the proposed development and the next step for the protesters."

"What do you expect?" Mort said, throwing his hands up. "I did the job of three people on deadline this morning, and that meeting ran late last night."

I understood his irritation. He'd already been on the hot seat with what had started as the lead story this morning; then, being the only person on deck, he'd probably caught the brunt of Lou's frustration, especially after I'd hung up on the man.

"Yeah, I feel your pain," Lou said. "Put some meat on it today. And don't give me a rewrite. I want something new."

"Maybe Vince could help me too," Maki said, with a false smile that exposed orange-stained gums. "C'mon, buddy. You've got the inside line on the protest, what with your wife running the show. How about it—what's next on the agenda?"

"You've got our number, Mort. Give her a call."

He snorted. "Seems like I've been down this road before."

"I think you ought to dig more into Jack Reynolds' motivation," I added. "Why's he pushing so hard for this project? Doesn't he have a conflict of interest? Especially since he's term-limited this fall, and you know his company's going to bid—"

"You're so transparent—"

"And what about the developer? Northstar Properties? You think it's a coincidence that it's owned by Reynolds' college roommate?"

"That's the same song your wife's crooning. The council didn't buy it."

"Enough," Lou growled. "He's got a point, Mort. Your story has to explore those issues. Okay, everybody—"

I interrupted. "What about the cemetery vandalism?"

Everyone who'd been turning to leave stopped.

"I didn't see anything in today's edition," I said. "The

chief mentioned it this morning, so it was probably on the dispatch log." I hoped I'd made a point that someone had failed to check the log. "Something about a mad backhoe driver digging up graves."

"I suppose I'll have to learn about that on television too," Lou groaned. "Vince, go get a couple photos, and do a brief on it for tomorrow. That's all we'll have room for, and I can't spare the photographer this afternoon."

"But—"

Lou's annoyed stare told me to keep my trap shut.

So much for my day off, I thought. I glanced at my watch. And so much for a little chat with the boss. If I took off now, I'd have just enough time to shoot the cemetery photos and still pick up Glory for our afternoon appointment.

Chapter Six

I drove the eight blocks to Apostle Bay's city cemetery, known locally as The Gardens. You'd think the name comes from the well-cultivated perennial beds throughout the grounds—maintained by a retired master gardener who can be found on-site throughout summer, poking, prodding, and snipping her way through foxglove, rudbeckia, and phlox—but it doesn't. Instead, it's a reference to the community vegetable gardens at a far end of the cemetery property. Area residents who have no space in their own yards, or at least no space conducive to producing vegetables in our short growing season, can rent a plot that's not yet needed for its intended purpose and plant something that will grow. It's kind of a communal hangout on summer evenings for Apostle Bay residents.

A black iron fence with spikes and curlicues surrounds The Gardens, and I drove through the only gate, an entrance that was closed for the first time in many years last spring when a young bull moose waded into one of the cemetery's two ponds, intent on clearing their vegetation. He was such an attraction, munching contentedly on lily pads, that the spectators who flocked to The Gardens each evening threatened to trample one another in their desire to get close enough for a photo—or, for that matter, to be trampled when the juvenile bull decided he'd had enough of humans pointing their camera phones at him.

By the third chaotic evening Aristotle Thanatos—the cemetery's ebullient caretaker, who leads after-hours birding tours around the grounds, and who once a month during the summer dresses in period costume and regales visitors with embellished tales of local history—had had enough. With a little help from the cops he herded everyone out and locked the gate. A couple days later the moose either ate his fill or lost interest in the cemetery as a home and moved on. Thanatos then reopened the graveyard to his regulars: power walkers, birders, and those visiting the dead.

I drove past the moose pond, the lily pads now turning autumn yellow, and followed the winding blacktop past a few strolling retirees out enjoying the fall colors. The road led me to the cemetery's center, where the trees were older, the shade deeper, and the city's first families lay beneath weathered, lichen-covered headstones. The fluttering yellow caution tape marked my destination—that and the John Deere backhoe and black pickup truck. I parked behind the truck and saw a worker picking through the destruction with a shovel. He stopped and watched me as I grabbed my camera from the passenger seat and climbed out.

The mess must have given Thanatos, fastidious as he is about his grounds, a near stroke. It looked as if a kid had been turned loose with the backhoe, cutting a swath of destruction some twenty yards long, knocking monuments off-kilter and churning grass and soil into a muddy mess. The vandalism culminated in a wide pit. Though no evidence was visible, it was obvious from the depth of the hole that the vandal had unearthed a handful of graves. Sandy loam was piled on the hole's far side, almost covering another memorial that bore fresh scars from the hoe's metal bucket.

"Hey," I said, waving to the worker. "What a mess, huh?"

He stood leaning on his shovel, a tall, barrel-chested man in jeans and a flannel shirt. He grunted, watching me from under the bill of a ball cap pulled low over a head that was either shaved or closely shorn. He didn't seem happy to see me. Either that or he didn't like poking around a grave site.

"I'm from the *Chronicle*," I said. "Don't mind me. I just came to get a few photos."

"Not of me," he said, lifting his shovel and moving away from the pit.

He pulled his cap lower and walked toward his truck, keeping some trees between us. I closed the gap as he ducked under the yellow tape and met him at the truck's tailgate as he tossed in the shovel. On closer inspection I decided he'd shaved his head.

"Any idea what happened here?"

"Nope," he said. He walked around the front of his vehicle and opened the door.

"Is Aristotle around?"

He answered me with a door slam and drove away.

"Friendly guy," I said.

I turned and snapped photos of the destruction, trying to catch an overall view. Then I ducked under the tape and walked toward the edge of the hole. Severed roots hung from the sides, and I glanced up at the massive hardwoods, wondering how much they'd been weakened.

I fired a couple photos of the hole and moved around the

edge toward the backhoe. It had an Apostle Bay decal on its side. The stabilizers were down and had gouged the earth, most likely while the hoe had been swinging back and forth during the excavation.

I moved around the equipment and on the opposite side found five headstones on the ground, placed side by side. Two were broken, the pieces set in place like those of a jig-saw puzzle. It looked as if a crew had already started the cleanup work—probably what that guy had been doing, sift-ing through the mess for pieces of headstones . . . or worse.

The monuments were weathered marble, white with gray streaks, softened by a century and a half of harsh winters and rain dripping from the trees. The lettering was faint but legible. The first stone, still intact, read:

MELVIN HAVER

1823–1854

GOD REST HIS SOUL

My knowledge of local history is a little weak, but I know that Melvin Haver was one of the first explorers to settle our town.

Lou'd probably want a full story now instead of a brief. I'd need to call our longtime county clerk, Monty Haver, too, get his feelings on the vandals disturbing his ancestors.

The marker next to Melvin's bore the name Charlotte Haver. Considering her birth date—1824—I assumed she was his wife. The two broken ones were for Randolph and Celeste. Both lived until the early 1900s.

I snapped photos of the gravestones, making sure I had a clear one of the broken monuments, and then took a few more shots of the entire scene, as much to remind myself of the details when I wrote about it as to get art for tomorrow's paper.

"Hey!" a woman's voice called. "Did they find who did this yet?"

Pushing a wheelbarrow across the road and heading toward me was Miriam Pohl, the green thumb who tends the cemetery's flower gardens. I'd written a feature on her the previous summer. She was a retired landscape architect from Philadelphia who settled in Apostle Bay to be near her grandchildren and who had—voluntarily and with her own funds—transformed the graveyard's perennial beds into a tourist attraction. Rumor was she and Aristotle had a thing going. If so, they seemed a perfect match: both extroverts, both high energy, and both committed to the cemetery's beauty.

"Hi, Miriam!" I called. I walked back around the hole to greet her.

Miriam parked her wheelbarrow; it was half full of deadheads she'd clipped back. She pulled off a work glove, tucked her short gray hair back under her gardening hat, and offered her hand when I was close enough.

"Who'd do something like this?" she said, nodding toward the vandalism. "It's senseless."

"What does Aristotle think?" I asked.

"He thinks it was a couple teens out joyriding."

"In a city backhoe? Where'd they get that?"

She nodded her head toward the far end of the cemetery. "From the community garden. Ari, the old fool, leaves it there at night, with the keys tucked into the visor in case one of the regulars needs to roll the compost or something."

"That's going to come back to bite him."

"Probably," she said. "Monty Haver wasn't too happy."

"Monty's seen this?"

"Oh, yes," she said. "Anyone on the grounds could hear him venting on Ari. You can see why he'd be upset."

We both turned to look at the damage again.

"How'd the vandals have time to make such a huge mess?" I asked. "Wouldn't Aristotle have heard them from the caretaker's house?"

"On most nights he might have," she answered. "But he was at the council meeting last night with just about everyone else in town, and then he went out for a nightcap."

"When did he discover it?"

"After he returned. Ari likes to cruise through the place one last time before he retires, just to check on things, make sure there aren't any kids hanging around or would-be lovers in parked cars. Whoever did this was already gone, but it was almost two."

"Were the . . . I mean . . ."

"Were the coffins opened? Yeah. Four of them, Vince. It wasn't pretty."

Chapter Seven

Miriam rolled the wheelbarrow toward her next flower bed, and I drove back to the caretaker's house.

Aristotle Thanatos lives in a quaint white cottage near the cemetery's entrance—a residence that would look more at home in a grove of red pine near a lake than adjacent to the cemetery's equipment barn.

I parked between Aristotle's electric golf cart and Monty Haver's white Lincoln Navigator. Haver's SUV gleamed with its usual polish.

From the cottage's little porch I heard shouting inside. The small suction-cup sign in the door said OPEN, so I twisted the handle and pushed through to find Monty and Thanatos going at it. They both stopped midsentence and shot me annoyed looks.

"Hey, guys," I said.

The office didn't boast much more than a cluttered wooden desk and two visitor chairs. Monty, though he's lost considerable weight in the last year, is a naturally big man and still a little on the soft side. Aristotle is built like a circus strongman and is so effusive in movement and manner that he seems to fill double the space of most humans.

The cramped room smelled of mud, leaves, diesel fuel, and sweat.

Monty was red faced. His usually impeccable attire was wrinkled, his collar open. He held a handkerchief in one hand and, after backing down from whatever he'd been about to say, mopped his forehead.

"Can I help you?" Aristotle asked.

"He's from the *Chronicle*," Monty said, a note of defeat in his voice. He dropped his bulk onto one of the visitor's seats.

"Oh, yeah, Doc's son," Aristotle said. "I remember chasing you out of here a few times when you were a kid."

"That was my evil twin," I quipped.

The burly Greek moved behind his desk and sat in a chair that creaked under his weight.

"I'm sorry, Monty," I said. "How're you doing?"

He waved a hand as if he didn't care.

"How do you think he feels?" Aristotle said. "His family's sacred ground has been desecrated. He's angry. He's furious. He's seething with rage!" Aristotle jumped up, knocking a few papers from his desk. "But we'll find who did this, these punks, these defilers who would disturb something sacrosanct not only to the family but to this entire community. It is an outrage."

He punctuated his last sentence by stepping toward me and shaking his finger.

"Any clues to who's responsible?" I asked.

"Punks, Rasputin-like villains who have no souls."

Well, that narrows it down, I felt like saying, but I bit my tongue and turned to Monty. "Who were Celeste and Randolph?"

"Melvin and Charlotte's children," he said. "Melvin was my great-great-grandfather."

"Do you think there's—"

"It's nothing more than a random act of savagery," Aristotle said. "Perpetrated by—"

"It wasn't the first time," Haver interrupted.

"He wants to move them," Aristotle said, pointing at Haver. "I keep telling him they belong here. His ancestors are a part of this city's history, a part of our lore. This is their rightful place."

"They've never really belonged," Haver said.

"How bad was the damage?" I asked.

Monty waved a hand again and dabbed his temples.

I turned to Aristotle.

"We think we found everything," he said.

"This wasn't the first time?"

"No," Haver said. "It wasn't."

"When?" I asked. "What happened before?"

"That was nothing," Aristotle said. "A long time ago. A Halloween prank, that's all. A minor event. Desecration, yes, but not on this scale. Nothing like this."

"You know that's not true," Haver said, rising out of his chair.

"Monty, Monty, we've been over this. Come now. I'm going to take care of your ancestors. I promise you. I give you my word, the word of Aristotle Thanatos, that your revered forebears will rest again and rest in peace."

"Monty?"

"Stupid rumors and stupid fools," he said. "I thought we were finally past this."

Haver came to the door, and I backed outside to let him pass. Without a glance he headed toward his SUV.

I followed, trying to make sense of what he'd said and wondering what I could say to ease his sorrow, but as soon as the words slipped out, I knew I'd said the wrong thing.

"Did you hear about the judge?"

"I did," he said, stopping at the door of his Navigator. He rested his forehead briefly on the SUV and closed his eyes. Then he turned to me, the anger so clear in his expression that I retreated a step. "And you know what I have to say? Good riddance. This is all his fault."

Chapter Eight

I was still puzzling over Monty Haver's final comment when Glory and I arrived at Lakeview Elder Care an hour later.

My daughter's surrogate grandmothers, excitement nearly bursting the seams of their party dresses, waited for us in the lobby. Behind the ladies festively tittering sat a receptionist, sighing, shaking her head, and acting altogether annoyed.

The ladies quieted when we approached. Diminutive Missy Blue, the undisputed queen, rolled forward in her wheelchair. My daughter, who in any other setting would have launched herself in a flying leap against the woman, stepped forward to meet her.

"Good afternoon, Missy Blue," she said. Her toddler voice was loud and formal. She curtsied with all the grace of an uncoordinated two-and-a-half-year-old.

The grannies, as best they could, did the same.

"Hello, Missy Blue," I said. "Sorry we're a few minutes late."

"Eleven minutes," she said with the abrupt tone I imagine

she used whenever the Lakeview staff got on her bad side. "And you smell like death." To Glory she said, "Shall we?"

I sniffed the air, wondering if I had somehow picked up an odor from the cemetery.

The ladies turned in unison toward the east wing corridor and resumed their spirited hand waving and chattering. Glory, a little princess in jeans and pink hoodie, peeked over one shoulder to make sure I wasn't following. This past summer Deb had joined the women on Glory's visits, as much for her own interest as to keep an eye on Glory. But my daughter had informed me, on multiple occasions, that the tea social was strictly a feminine affair, and Deb, now comfortable with the ladies, gave the okay.

Glory and I met Missy Blue a little over a year ago when I was at Lakeview to interview a resident named Waino Toivola. At the time I'd been dragging Glory on a wild goose chase around town, and she'd been midtantrum when we passed through the lobby doors. Missy Blue's intervention with tissues and a cookie was a godsend.

My daughter ended up in Missy's room, playing with Barbies the elderly woman kept for her absentee grandchildren, while I interviewed Waino.

Missy Blue tracked us down a month later and invited Glory back. And while she's never warmed to me, she treats our daughter as a cherished grandchild.

In recent months Glory's weekly visits to Lakeview have evolved into a major social happening. An expanding cast of ladies now have their hair done and break out formal dress for the event. They all spend an hour spoiling our daughter and teaching her how to act like a princess. I was still on the fence about whether this was a good idea, but that didn't matter, since I had the minority vote.

With Glory and her group headed toward tea, I circled past the receptionist, who now had her face buried in a romance novel and was no doubt enjoying the lobby's return to morguelike silence.

Off the lobby is a glass-walled waiting room with dreadful ochre-colored chairs circa 1970, a television, and some end tables with books and lamps. I settled myself in the room, nodding to the lone occupant seated opposite me. He was a lanky man, swimming inside a burnt-orange polyester leisure suit much too large for his skeletal frame. He'd rolled the sleeves back to his forearms and was flipping through a magazine.

He smiled my way, flashing dark, stained teeth.

I opened my laptop, connected the camera, and set to work proving I could still crank out material—knowing that was exactly what Lou'd hoped to achieve with his earlier tirade questioning my commitment.

While the cemetery photos loaded onto my computer, I called Gord. I wanted to hear his thoughts on the vandalism and see if there was any news about the judge's death, but he was out. I left a message for him to call my cell.

When I closed the phone, Leisure Suit came across the room and sat two chairs to my left. I forced a polite but what I hoped wasn't a welcoming smile his way. He curled his lips back like a horse, offering a view of his incisors. I did a double take, squinting for a better look.

"Ya like these babies?" he said, pointing to his teeth. I had trouble understanding him because of the way he held his lips open.

Each of his top four teeth was a miniature replica of an American flag. I couldn't help myself and leaned in for a closer view.

"Interesting," I said.

"Actually got all fifty stars on 'em if ya look through a magnifying glass. Here, check 'em out."

He pulled out his denture and held it out toward me. I leaned away.

"Thanks anyway."

"Go ahead. Check it out."

"I'll pass."

"They're new," he said, after reinserting the false teeth. "Ya can get all kinds of stuff on 'em these days. Kind of makes a statement, don't you think?"

"Indeed," I said. "Maybe you should get matching contact lenses for your eyes. They might let you be Grand Marshal in the Fourth of July parade."

"Ya really think so?" he asked.

I shrugged. "Why not?"

My pictures finished loading. I disconnected the camera and then scrolled through them, taking another look at the vandalism. Something about the mess bothered me. It seemed sloppy but clearly targeted those specific graves. The vandal had trampled other sites just to set up and dig in this spot. The fact that the outriggers were set convinced me the person had had a specific goal.

Leisure Suit moved next to me and leaned in front of my face to check out the photos. "Whatcha lookin' at?"

"Some photos. Do you mind? I need to get some work—"

"Looks like the cemetery," he interrupted.

"Yeah. Excuse me. I need to make a call."

I moved my gear to the opposite side of the room, flipped open my cell phone, and called the county clerk's office. I needed more info from Monty about this and the earlier vandalism.

Deputy Clerk Rhonda Wentworth, queen of Superior County gossip, answered.

"Hey, Vince," she said. She offered the bare minimum of pleasantries and then asked, "Got anything good you can share about the judge?"

"I'm sure you know more than I. In fact, I called Monty for a few more details on a peripheral story. Is he around?"

Her voice dropped to a whisper. "He's got the cops in his office."

I found myself whispering too. "About the cemetery vandalism?"

"Nah, that was—"

A loud blast of noise from the TV drowned out the rest of her words. Leisure Suit held the remote. He smiled at me.

"Can you turn it down please?" I asked him. I covered my free ear and said to Rhonda, "Sorry, you'll have to speak up."

"I said he met with them this morning about, you know, someone digging up his ancestors," she said. "Right now they're here—"

The TV's volume went a notch louder. Leisure Suit fumbled with the remote as if he'd cranked it by accident, but I could tell he was gauging my reaction. I moved into the lobby, closing the lounge door as I left. The receptionist looked up from her book and glowered.

"It's not me," I told her.

"Are you calling from a football stadium?" Rhonda asked.

"The nursing home."

"The nursing home? What's going on, a revolt?

"It's nothing. Why are the cops there?"

"They're talking to him about the judge."

"Who is?"

"Chief Weathers and that handsome detective."

Handsome? That ruled out Freeman.

"Makes sense," I said. "Monty and the judge worked closely together."

"Not really." Her voice was still a whisper. "I handled everything with Judge Sorenson because Monty, well . . . there was some bad blood between those two."

"I thought everybody loved the judge."

"Definitely not Monty," she said. "They think he might have killed him."

"Get real," I said. I noticed that inside the lounge Leisure Suit had turned off the TV and was waving at me through the window.

"I'm serious, Vince. Didn't you hear about the big blowup last week? I tried to keep it quiet, but half the county staff heard it. I swear Monty and the judge were going at it so loudly, the windows were rattling."

"About what?"

"I don't know. I heard Monty say something about dredging up the past again. But he wouldn't tell me when I asked, and you know that's strange. We're tight. Oops, gotta go."

She cut me off. Rhonda's a great source when it comes to court documents because she has a computerlike mind, but she's also a world-class rumormonger, and I've learned it's prudent to check her stories when they aren't backed up by county documents.

"Hey, you." Leisure Suit stood in the open doorway, holding my laptop in one arm. "When did ya take these pictures?" he asked.

I crossed to him in three quick steps and grabbed the computer.

"I'd appreciate it if—"

"Them's the Haver graves, aren't they?" he said.

"Yeah, they are. Someone trashed them last night."

I moved into the room, deciding the only way to get clear of this guy was to pack up and head out to my car. Glory'd be here another half hour, so I could still make a couple calls and bang out a vandalism story. Lou could edit it down to a brief if that's all he wanted.

"Ain't the first time that's happened," Leisure Suit said, following me into the room so closely that I could smell the mothballs his burnt-orange duds had been stored in.

"Is that so?" I wondered if he was talking about the Halloween prank Aristotle had mentioned.

"Yeah, someone dug up those graves when I was a kid," he said. He stepped over to the door and pulled it closed. I started to object but stopped when he said, "I know who done it."

"You do, huh? And who would that be?"

He looked over one shoulder, glanced around the room, then whispered, "It was my, um, my friend."

"I see."

"Don't ya believe me?"

"Not exactly. But just for kicks I'll ask, why'd your friend do something like that?"

"For the money," he whispered.

"The money?"

"Yeah, you know. *The money.* Nobody ever did find it after he killed hisself. They say his wife buried it with him."

I glanced at my watch and decided that by the time I got out of here, I wouldn't get much done anyway. And this guy was as intriguing as he was annoying. I pointed toward a chair.

"Okay," I said. "Why don't you sit down and tell me all about it?"

Chapter Nine

"What's your name?" I asked when he'd lowered his backside into a chair and leaned forward, elbows on his knees, smiling a big patriotic smile, glad for my attention.

"Junior."

"Junior . . . ?"

"Junior Ross."

"And you live here, Mr. Ross?"

"No way. Just visiting." He showed the flags again. "I come to see Phil."

"So tell me all about this grave-robbing friend of yours."

"Weren't exactly grave robbery," he said. " 'Cause nothing got taken. It weren't there."

"Your friend couldn't find the coffin?"

"No. Couldn't find the loot."

"Ah . . . Maybe you ought to start at the beginning," I said. "What loot?"

"You know," he said, grabbing his head with both hands

as if my ignorance was giving him a migraine. "The money that Apostle guy stole."

"O-o-o-kay."

"This is what I—uh, I mean, what my friend told me. This Haver guy stole a bunch a money way back when Apostle Bay was just beginning. And he got caught. Then he killed hisself, but no one found the money. So's, uh, my friend, he figures—this is way back now, probably the sixties or so— he figures Haver's family hid it in the coffin, you know, buried him with it, so's—" Until now, Junior had been sitting a safe distance across the room from me, but he moved into the chair next to mine and whispered, "—So's he dug up the body. Took him all night, but the money weren't there. Just bones."

He leaned back, his wide eyes conspiratorial, as if this all made a load of sense. I wish I'd thought to record him.

"Just bones?" I said. "You're saying that back in the 1960s this friend of yours dug up Melvin Haver's grave and opened the coffin, looking for money Haver supposedly stole that was never recovered?"

He nodded and smiled. "Ain't no 'supposedly.' He stole it, all right—I mean, according to the stories."

"Did he rob a bank?"

"No. He stole it from his company. What do they call it— he embedded it?"

"Embezzled?"

"Yeah, that's it."

"I see. So what did your friend do? After he discovered there were only bones in the coffin?"

Junior leaned really close, giving me another close-up of his dentures and a good whiff of coffee breath.

"He buried him again," he whispered. Then he sat back proudly. "I ain't no criminal or nothing."

"I see. *You're* not a criminal?"

"No, sir," he said, sitting taller, crossing his heart, and holding up a three-fingered salute that I supposed was some form of pledge.

"Tell me more about this suicide," I said.

Junior looked at me incredulously. "Everybody knows he done hung himself. Right down by the Manitou."

Ah, the historical suicide Ashley had mentioned. I started to ask him for details, but a nurse's aide opened the glass door.

"Excuse me," she said. She smiled at me in that way people do when they're saying sorry you had to go through this, and then she turned to Junior. "Phil, it's time for dinner."

"How many times I got to tell you, lady? I'm Junior." He grabbed his head with both hands again. "I'm here to *visit* Phil."

"I'm sorry. Excuse me, Junior," she said. She gave me a wink. "It's time to come on back and join Phil for dinner."

"What's he having?"

"Yankee pot roast and mashed potatoes tonight."

"That sounds good," Junior said, rising to his feet, calm again. He straightened his polyester coat, picked a piece of lint from the lapel and flicked it into the air, then followed her out of the room. Apparently he'd forgotten me. I noticed the aide held his arm as they left.

I watched them disappear down the corridor, and then I went to the lobby reception desk.

"Who was that man in the lounge with me?"

"Him? Oh, that's Phil Ross," the receptionist answered. "He hangs out in that lounge every afternoon."

"He said his name was Junior."

"Phil Ross, Jr. It's pathetic really. He tells everyone his name is Junior and that he's here to visit Phil. I think it's because he never has any real visitors, so he visits himself."

"I see. And just how, uh, lucid is Phil?"

She snorted, then answered, "Him? He's completely bonkers."

When I slipped into the common room to pick up Glory from the tea soiree, you'd have thought I was the worst scoundrel in Michigan from all the evil glares directed my way. *How'd I screw up now?* I wondered.

An aide pulled me aside as Glory said her good-byes.

"Look, I don't want to intrude on your personal life," she said, "but I just can't help myself in this matter. When your daughter was playing with the dolls, she kept wrapping Barbie's boa around Ken's neck and hanging him from things. It got the ladies rather upset—"

"You're letting her watch too much TV," Missy Blue interrupted. I hadn't noticed her roll up behind me. "Too much violence," she said. "She needs tea parties, dolls, and make-believe. She needs books and that purple dinosaur thing. People want to know why there's so much violence in the world. It's because—"

"It's because there aren't enough grandmothers like you," I said, bending down and scooping Glory up into my arms. "Thank you, Missy Blue. You're absolutely right."

And maybe you'll understand better this evening when you watch the news, I thought.

Chapter Ten

By the time we rolled out of Lakeview's parking lot, Glory was snoozing in her car seat. I knew I had a late night ahead, so I pulled over at a convenience store, ran in, and bought a caffeine-loaded energy drink that was guaranteed to boost my IQ and stamina. Then I tried Monty Haver again, but both he and Rhonda were gone for the day. Monty didn't answer at his home either.

I called the Apostle Bay Historical Society, hoping to catch archivist Patrice Berklee. If anyone in town knew the Haver family dirt, it would be the former Michigan State history professor who'd retired here and devoted her life to organizing our local historic documents. She was gone for the day too, but I'd catch her at class tonight. We were both taking a kayak safety course at the high school pool.

My plan for when we got home was to let Glory sleep—in the Bronco, if necessary—while I got a jump on my stories. I needed to write the piece about the cemetery vandalism, including info about the previous incident, crank out something on the process to replace the judge, and I still owed Ashley an e-mail with the judge's background.

That plan went out the window, however, when I saw my full driveway and the fleet of cars parked in front of our little bungalow.

Deb, Glory, and I live in a cedar-shake cabin about a mile north of the Manitou River and a few miles south of a popular granite outcrop called Eagle's Cliff. Our home was once my parent's summer place. Mom improved the cabin for year-round use—insulating and adding a furnace—when we decided to move here from Grand Rapids several years back. It's a small house, hardly enough space for a family of three. Every winter we debate if we can stand another four or five months of biting arctic wind that somehow wends through tiny crevices and cracks in the cabin's walls and chills us despite the furnace. But each summer, campfires on the Lake Superior beach, a chance to splash in the pristine shallows, and the spectacular view out our kitchen window convince us to stay.

That may change with the Explorer's Park development, Deb says. She's convinced the condos will not only be visible from our beach but will also bring a swarm of annoying personal watercraft buzzing past our home all summer. This is the reason she's devoted so much time to SCALD—Superior Citizens Against Lakeshore Development.

I parked on our lawn behind the giant plywood sign showing a red circle with slash through a picture of a high-rise building. Sarah Dodge, a local attorney who'd represented Deb last year when she was mistakenly arrested on a drug charge, walked around the house, waved, and veered my way. Deb told me last night that Sarah agreed to represent

SCALD in their attempt to stop the development. The judge, before his death, had agreed to foot the bill.

"Who do you think killed him?" she asked in the demanding way she talks whether she's asking questions in court or sitting at your table asking for the pepper.

I pointed at Glory sleeping in the backseat, put a finger to my lips, and eased the door closed. We stepped away from the Bronco.

"I don't think the cops have ruled out suicide," I said.

"Yeah, right. Do they have any suspects yet? What's your take? I heard you discovered the body."

"Let's see: Yes, if you believe the rumors; I'm still evaluating; and not exactly."

"Who? Why? And how can you 'not exactly' discover a dead guy hanging from a tree?"

"Monty Haver. Not enough info. Not the first one there."

"Really?" she said, her left eyebrow arching above her black glasses frame, the only sign she was surprised at this information. "I'd heard about Monty's big blowout with the judge, but he's not a killer. No way. You said it's just rumor? Must be Rhonda's work. So who was there first?"

"Wow, you're quick," I said. "Yes, it was Rhonda. And Ashley Adams was there first."

"Your replacement? Pure luck, or someone tip her off?"

"Smart money is she had a tip. Who do you think killed him?"

"Someone convicted in his court."

"You think? With his reputation for giving everyone a break?"

"Not everyone," Sarah said.

I realized she was the perfect person to know this because

she spent more time defending locals in Superior County Circuit Court than just about anyone else.

"You have someone in mind?"

"Not a particular person. Check his domestic violence cases. That was his pet peeve, and he came down hard on those convicted. And you know how some of the folks around here think: the cops and courts shouldn't get involved in something that's between a man and his property."

The bitterness in those last two words was understandable, considering her own background, something we'd been learning in bits and pieces since she and Deb became friends after last year's fiasco.

"Gotta run, Vince. Let me know if you turn up something."

She spun and headed toward her car.

"Hey, Sarah!" I called. "You know this leaves only Freeman running for the court in November. A woman judge could help change that attitude."

"Doubtful," she said over one shoulder.

Chapter Eleven

I left Glory asleep in her car seat, knowing she'd wake if I moved her, and wandered around our bungalow to the lake side. There I found half dozen new yard signs: DON'T SELL OUT OUR COMMUNITY, SAVE EXPLORER'S PARK, etc. They were shiny with wet paint and leaning against our small deck.

Two of Deb's students from Bay High added finishing touches to some foam-board posters. Deb, dark hair pulled back in a short ponytail, her arms and Michigan Tech sweat-shirt splattered with red and white paint, cleaned brushes in a bucket while chatting with a few animated SCALD members.

She smiled when she saw me—a small gesture that said hi, and we're almost done here, and I've had a wonderful day. It's one of her traits that's always awed me, the way she can share so much information with a glance and grin. Her friends waved and said hi.

"How's Glory?" Deb asked.

"Fine," I said. "They wore her out at tea. She's asleep in the car. What's going on here? I thought the protests were over after last night."

"Not by a long shot," she said. Her voice sounded more enthusiastic than I'd expected after last night's vote and now the judge's death. "Our answering machine was packed with messages today, and it was the same for other SCALD members. I think a lot of people woke up last night when the council approved the development. We've doubled our unofficial membership, and people are already contributing money for the legal defense. We're just getting started, Vince."

"I can see," I said, nodding at the signs.

I went in through our back door, deposited my laptop and camera on the kitchen table, and came back out to check on Glory.

The SCALDers were clearing out. I helped carry a few of the dry signs around front and loaded them into cars. A quick peek into my Bronco showed Glory still snoozing.

Deb thanked each person, waited for the last car to pull away, then came over to me and said, "When I asked you how Glory was doing earlier, I meant how was she doing about finding the judge? How's she taking it?"

"Well, Missy Blue said she was strangling Ken dolls with Barbie's boa."

"That's great."

"Yeah. I already got the lecture. But really, Deb, I don't think she has a clue as to what she saw."

I'd left Deb a message at school about our morning because I knew she'd hear about it from someone else during the day. Now I filled her in on the details.

"So much for this sleepy little town you said would be a good place to raise children," she said.

My attempt to move Glory inside without waking her was unsuccessful. She went from comatose silence to tears and flailing between the car and house—understandable, considering her strange day and the fact I'm sure she was starving. Deb got some applesauce and crackers into her and talked about the tea party while I heated soup and toast.

Afterward Deb gave Glory a bath and snuggled with her on the couch while I searched my laptop for past stories about the judge that I could e-mail Ashley. I didn't have much to offer because major crimes or high-profile civil suits are rare here. Then again, Ashley said she didn't need my help. I flirted with keeping the Monty Haver rumor to myself—the fact that he was a suspect and the stuff about his family's graves—but, knowing I'd expect her to share such information with me, I passed it along.

Deb came into the kitchen as I was sending the note.

"Glory's down," she said. She dropped into a chair beside me and started pulling papers from her briefcase.

"So what's the next step for SCALD?" I asked. "You have another demonstration at city hall scheduled?"

"A memorial for Judge Sorenson," she said.

"With picket signs? Don't you think that's a little . . . oh, I don't know . . . crass?"

"No," she said. "The judge was dead set against this development. And it was his family's land. We think it's appropriate. Besides, it's not a protest. We're going to have a candlelight vigil tomorrow night at Explorer's Park, a silent walk through the park, and then a eulogy at the Apostle

Memorial. Do you think the *Chronicle* will give us some coverage?"

"Call Maki."

Deb rolled her eyes as if that would be a waste of time. Even though he was doing his job last year, she still blames him for the embarrassing coverage of when she and a coworker were arrested after someone had framed them for drug possession.

"It's his beat, Deb. And he was whining today that he didn't have enough information to write a follow-up story, so maybe he'd be glad for something."

"He writes about SCALD like we're a bunch of crack-pots—"

"Deb, you're exaggerating."

"Stop defending him," she said. "I don't want to bad-mouth the *Chronicle,* Vince, 'cause I know you love that place, but that guy, he's . . . he's . . . ah—"

"Okay, forget Maki. Why don't you call Lucy DeMott? You get the TV covering it, the newspaper will follow. Lou can't stand getting scooped by the TV—doesn't even matter if it's not real news."

I saw my e-mail was sent, so I logged off and reconnected our phone line. Someday our little town may advance to cable modems or wireless.

"I still can't believe the council voted to go forward with those condos," Deb said. "It's so obviously not within the intent of the Sorenson family gift."

"Maybe the protest backfired, Deb. I'd guess Jack Reynolds got a few council members all riled up. You know, 'Don't be swayed by a bunch of liberal, granola-crunching elitists—"

"I hate granola, and we're not liberal elitists—"

"I know. But I'll bet Reynolds played it that way. He probably convinced them that you terrible tree huggers were trying to ram your opinion down their throats, and, 'We can't stand for that, blah, blah, blah.' I'll bet two or three of the councilmen only voted Jack's way because he got their hackles up, not because they believe it's the right thing."

"Why can't people see through that man?" Deb asked. "The guy's obviously going to profit from this. At least he shouldn't have been allowed to vote last night."

"Wouldn't have made a difference. He had the majority."

"We'll stop it in court," she said. "This is not why the land was given to the city."

"I wonder: if you do file, who'll hear the case? That's one of the things either Mort or I need to include in our stories."

"Right now I'm more concerned about who'll replace the judge as our funding source. Even with the contributions today and Sarah Dodge doing some of the legwork pro bono, it's still going to cost."

"Why don't you try the judge's nephew? His name's Peter Sorenson. Find out if he'll honor his uncle's commitment. Ashley said he's the judge's sole heir."

"I don't have high hopes for that. Rumor is he's been riding around town in Jack Reynolds' hip pocket."

"How'd Reynolds swing that? Stop by the house before the judge's body was cold?"

"Even sooner," Deb said. "Jack's been wining and dining him behind the judge's back most of the summer."

"Where'd you hear that?"

"People in SCALD who work for nonprofits. Some of them have long-term pledges from the judge for funding, and they're worried things might change."

"If Peter Sorenson is seeing our community through the eyes of Jack Reynolds, then someone better make sure he gets another view," I said.

"I know. But don't you think it's tacky to contact him now? I mean, shouldn't we at least wait until after the funeral?"

"You're competing with Jack Reynolds, Deb."

"That doesn't mean I'm going to act like him. We'll find another way if we have to. Maybe with the membership growing, we'll be okay. The judge seemed confident last night that we'd win the battle if it went to court."

"Overconfident," I said.

"No one really believes he killed himself, do they?"

I shrugged.

"I'll bet it has something to do with the development. You should tell the chief to look at Jack."

"I don't 'tell' my godfather anything, Deb. You know that."

"Get your mom to tell him. She's got his ear."

I rolled my eyes. The chief's been my mother's self-appointed guardian since Dad died—as if she needs one.

"I'll see Jack in a little while," I said. "Maybe I'll share your suspicions, just to tweak him."

Chapter Twelve

Hanging upside down in the water gives you a new perspective on the world, particularly when you're struggling to right yourself and your lungs feel as if they're about to climb out your throat in search of relief. When that happens, when the adrenaline kicks in, all those little life annoyances like deadlines and bosses and tantrums are forgotten in the quest for survival.

I'm pretty good at flipping my sea kayak, a sixteen-foot, low-riding plastic boat not much wider than my hips. Indeed, I may be the expert at the first half of what's often called an Eskimo roll. My problem is, once I'm upside down, I can't seem to throw my hips with the correct Elvis-like swivel needed to right myself. Our instructor calls it a *C*-to-*C* move. I can't figure out how to achieve the second *C*.

The worst part is that not being able to flip topside means yanking off the neoprene spray skirt, swimming out of the cockpit, and surfacing in front of my classmates with a loud gasp. And, of course, manually flipping the kayak and spending another five minutes trying to get all the water out. For me it also means the added embarrassment of being the last student in the class to solve this problem.

Which is why with each failure I persevere longer than I should, preferring the lung-searing pain of asphyxiation to the looks of pity—or in one case, scorn—on the faces of my classmates.

This time, I vowed, would be it. Everyone else had popped at least one *C*-to-*C*. Even the retired doctor and his wife, two people who looked too frail to paddle, much less gyrate their knees and hips to flip their vessel. Jack Reynolds, a self-acknowledged expert on everything, flipped so well, I swear his moussed hair didn't get wet.

This time I had a cheat. I was using a paddle float, an inflatable yellow bag that fits over the end of my paddle to give it increased buoyancy and, theoretically, allows me to lever myself up with arm strength instead of style.

I hung in there. I thrashed and made *C* shapes. I reset my body. I flailed my paddle and swiveled until I was so dizzy from the gyrations and lack of oxygen, I forgot which way was up, and when I finally struggled from the cockpit, I dove straight for the pool bottom, jamming a finger before turning around and bursting through the surface.

"What were you doing down there?" Reynolds asked, his voice reverberating off the pool's high ceiling. "Fighting the Loch Ness monster?"

"Had a spider in my cockpit," I said after gulping a few lungfuls of air. "Dang thing was tickling me."

That got a few laughs from the rest of the class and a delayed chuckle from Reynolds. I guess he didn't want to seem like too much of a jerk.

"It's just a matter of timing, Vince," the instructor said, yet again. I noticed he was closer to me than when I'd gone upside down and that everyone else had moved across the pool. He'd probably come to rescue me while the others were moving away from fear I'd take them down too. "One day you'll get it and then wonder why you struggled."

"That's about it for tonight, folks," he said. "Only a couple of days until our full-moon paddle on the lake. We'll meet at Benoit Beach. Remember, wet suits and PFDs are mandatory. Lake Superior has two temperatures: ice and melted ice. You fall in next week, and you've got ten, maybe fifteen minutes before you start losing motor skills. Maybe a half hour until you lose consciousness. After that, you're fish food."

"You're exaggerating," Reynolds said. "People swim in the lake all summer."

"No, people splash around and play in Lake Superior," he said. "You'll notice they don't stay immersed. Water is a heat vacuum, Jack. It sucks all the warmth out of you. When you're neck deep in Superior, you're in water that's forty or fifty degrees colder than your body. You'd have a better chance of survival standing in a blizzard in your skivvies. And those beach swimmers? They don't need the motor skills to right their boat or to climb back in without tipping again—you will."

"What good are wet suits if it's that cold?" the doctor's wife asked.

"They buy you time," our instructor told her. "When hypothermia sets in, your body shuts down the blood flow to your fingers and toes to save your organs. If you delay that, your hands work a little longer, and you can get yourself out of the water. That's another reason not to go solo—a partner can help when your fingers go numb."

In the locker room I showered and dressed quickly, conscious that I still had a chunk of work to complete before morning. Since my main reason for coming tonight had not been to suck water up my nose, but rather to talk with Patrice, her absence was a major disappointment.

While packing my bag I watched Jack Reynolds, clad in his black Speedo brief, tanned and waxed and puffed up like a steroid advertisement, telling the retired doctor what a great investment a condo on the Manitou River would be. The doctor offered a smile that looked more like a desperate grimace and squeezed around Reynolds, mumbling something noncommittal.

I packed the last wet stuff into my bag and turned to leave too. Reynolds caught me at the door. He stood six inches taller than I and got a little too much into my space.

"Exciting day in Apostle Bay," he said.

"Yep," I said.

"I'm not surprised about the judge, you know. Between you and me, that information about his, ah . . . proclivities, was going to come to light soon."

"It was?" This guy was so transparent about wanting me to believe this, I decided to egg him on to see what he'd say. I set my bag on the ground, zipped it open, and pulled out a reporter's notebook and pen. "How do you know that?"

Reynolds took a step back when he saw the notebook. I watched his eyes narrow and thought it funny how a little pad of paper could put a big, intimidating guy on the defensive.

"I was speaking off the record."

"That's okay," I said. "I'm just taking notes for background.

So, you were saying you knew something about the judge's private life that was going to become public soon?"

"I never said that."

"Oh, I must have misunderstood you."

I stared, pen poised, waiting for him to elaborate. He tried to wait me out, but politicians never can. They have some genetic need to babble.

"The Explorer's Park development is going to create jobs for this community. Now that it's moving forward, we need to pull together and get everyone onboard."

"The judge sure was adamant that your condo development didn't meet the requirements of his family's gift. Good thing he's dead, because I don't think he'd ever be 'onboard.' Do you think his death saved the city and the developer a protracted legal battle?"

"What's that supposed to mean?" Reynolds asked.

"Do the city and developer benefit from the judge's death?"

"I'm not going to answer that."

"Why not?"

I watched him take a deep breath and measure his words.

"The city council approved the Explorer's Park development plan. We're doing what's best for our city's residents."

"I see."

"How come you didn't write that down?"

"I have a good memory. Is your contracting company going to bid on the project?"

"I've already answered that. We'll have to see the plans before we decide. That's a private business decision."

"But you've been working with Northstar Properties, helping them with construction estimates. Isn't that a conflict of interest? Your being the mayor at the same time?"

"I've already answered that too," Reynolds said. "But I'd be happy if the *Chronicle* published my response. I've donated my expertise as a contractor to help plan this project. It's meant a huge savings to the city, and I've been able to keep the council's hand in the planning process through every step. That's why the council approved the development last night. Because we all knew it was the best plan for Apostle Bay."

"And you won't be the mayor in another two months, so you can bid on the project, right?"

He lowered his voice. "Did your wife put you up to this?"

"My wife? You cornered me, Jack. I was on my way out of here."

"I was just making conversation."

"Get real, Jack. You never just make conversation. There's a motive to everything you do."

"Touchy, touchy," he said. "Your wife's really got you under her thumb on this."

"My wife is a better judge of character than I am."

I stuffed my notebook back into my bag, hefted it over one shoulder, and reached for the door.

"You'd better tell her to keep SCALD under control," he said, his tone almost a whisper.

I let go of the door handle and got into *his* face. "Are you threatening Deb?"

"Let's just say there are some people looking forward to the jobs this development is going to bring to our community, and they might not take kindly to a group of tree huggers causing trouble. You never know what some people might do."

I pulled out my notebook again and scribbled some words on it as if I was taking his quote. "You're right, Jack—you never know what some people might do."

"If you—" I heard him say, but I was out the door, happy to get in the last word—this time.

Chapter Thirteen

A bad habit I picked up from my father is sleeplessness. I can't leave work at the door, and I sometimes spend the night stewing over a story or over the day's events.

Dad was a general practitioner when he lived. I often wonder if he was the only physician in Apostle Bay at one point. Hardly a week goes by without someone telling me Doc delivered their child, removed their tonsils, or stitched them up. His patients and their various ailments consumed his thoughts. Even when he was tossing a ball with me or eating Sunday dinner or shoveling snow, you could see that his mind was somewhere else. His answers to my questions were sometimes so off-the-wall, I knew he hadn't been listening, and he once cleared a path through the snow from our porch to the neighbor's driveway instead of our own.

As a kid, when I woke in the middle of the night with a full bladder or a bad dream, I'd see the light from his desk lamp leaking out the bottom of his closed office door. On the few occasions I pushed the door open, Dad would be writing, or just staring at the ceiling, looking for the answer to some problem in the white, stippled drywall.

I'm trying to overcome those habits, for Glory's sake and my own. And I feel it's necessary to prove to Deb that I can walk away from the work. After all, I don't even bring the police scanner into our bedroom anymore.

However, I knew heading to bed after kayak class would have been pointless. I logged an hour searching the Internet for state law regarding how to replace a dead judge, and I banged out my graveyard story. I kept wondering about Monty's comments too.

Glory has the same aversion to sleep, so I was annoyed but not surprised that she cried out during a potty break I was taking from my research. I stuck my head into her room.

"Get up?" she asked, standing in her crib, holding her stuffed frog under one arm and looking ready to romp.

"No, honey. It's still sleepy time." My watch said 4:00 A.M.

She cocked her head as if considering this, then, to my surprise, dropped back into her crib.

What a tease. She waited until I was three steps away, let me believe I'd won, then cut loose with a wicked screech.

The Laughing Whitefish Cafe overlooks the harbor and is within walking distance of the ore dock, a massive, elevated structure where railcars drop loads of iron pellets the size of garbanzo beans down chutes and into the holds of ore ships. The cafe opens at 5:00 A.M., ready to serve hot beef sandwiches smothered in rich gravy to the railroad guys getting off the night shift, their clothes stained red from ore dust. For those early birds heading into work it's grease-sizzled bacon and eggs and toast dripping with butter.

Glory and I climbed onto our usual stools at the counter,

the ones closest to the cash register so she could greet the other regulars. The waitress slid two chocolate milks and two humongous sticky buns in front of us. The pastries are close to the size of Glory's head. Neither of us can eat an entire one, but my independent daughter feels she must have her own, and I acquiesce because I'm a softy. I save the leftovers for Mort Maki or the cops at city hall.

I picked at mine and listened to the buzz about Judge Sorenson while Glory found a way to coat her hands, face, and hair with brown goo while firing a regular stream of questions at me. Each answer I gave resulted in several follow-up questions, until I'd lost track of the original thread. I sometimes think I'm nothing more than a human Web page to her, with hyperlinks she can follow at her whim.

I appreciated that the morning regulars didn't ask us about discovering the judge, although I know they were dying to do so. Something about the red-eye crowd at the Laughing Whitefish: they respect your personal space. I can't say the same thing applies later in the day.

Detective Captain Gordon Greenleaf strolled in at his usual quarter to six, got a sticky high five from Glory, and ordered a grilled egg-and-cheese on sourdough to go.

"Don't you guys ever sleep?" he asked, dropping onto the stool next to mine with the subtle grin he wore when off duty. On the clock, Gord was serious and focused, just as he was on the football field in high school. I envy the way he can switch it on and off like that.

"Nah, we'd rather be causing trouble," I said.

"You aren't kidding. My job was pretty boring 'til you came back to town and brought Deb with you."

"Glad we could accommodate. Making any progress on yesterday's events?"

"No comment," he said. He leaned in front of me and stuck his tongue out at Glory. She giggled.

"I heard an interesting story yesterday," I said.

The waitress handed Greenleaf a foil-wrapped sandwich. He moved to the cash register and paid. While waiting for his change, he said, "Do I really want to hear it?"

I shrugged. "It's entertaining."

"Okay. Why don't you two come on over when you're done here?"

I checked my watch. "I'm dropping Glory off at my mom's in half an hour. How about after that?"

"I'll brew the coffee."

"Sounds like a threat," I said as he headed out the door.

Chapter Fourteen

Gail Stevens, the police department's rail-thin administrative assistant, buzzed me through security when I arrived at city hall. Gail has twenty years on me, is twice as fit, and has a voice that's been rubbed raw by too many subzero training runs.

We chatted about her latest marathon, a fifty-mile ultra, and about Glory. I told her Gordon expected me.

"Not here to check the dispatch log?" she asked.

"Nah. I miss our daily chats, but I'm a part-timer now. Ashley Adams is covering this beat."

"You think so?"

I gave her a noncommittal shrug and headed past her desk to the detectives' offices.

I found Gordon sitting behind his desk, watching a slide show. He waved me in and at the same time killed the power to his monitor.

"The judge's house?" I asked, nodding to the now dark screen.

He smiled and told me to pour myself a cup of sludge from his coffeepot.

"What did you find there?"

"I thought you were here to entertain me," he said.

"Don't worry, Gord. I'm not on the story. That's Ashley's assignment, and, believe me, she's made it quite clear she's handling it all on her own."

"Yeah, she told me yesterday," he said. "She didn't seem to understand that I was interviewing her, not the other way around."

"Did you get out of her why she happened to be at the park?"

"She claims she was just out for a morning stroll."

"Get real. She was tipped off."

"If so, we'll find out," Gord said. "I have a subpoena to pull her phone records—both her home and cell phones. She didn't elicit much trust with us yesterday."

"But she did get a heck of a story. You're not seriously considering this as a suicide, are you?"

"I thought you're not working this story."

"I'm curious."

"That's your problem. You're too curious." He looked at his door, seemed to consider something, then said, "Mind if we close the door?"

We had an agreement. Anything he told me once the door was shut had to stay inside the room. I was free to decline—I usually did, because he might tell me something I'd discover another way, and then I'd be in a tough spot—but I was still torqued about yesterday, and since I really wasn't on the story, what did it matter?

"Go ahead," I said.

Gord stepped around the desk and closed the door. Then he sat back down and turned on his monitor. It was still cycling through the photos, images of a house interior.

"The judge's house?"

"Yeah."

The pictures flowed across his screen, showing what appeared to be an office or library. Papers were strewn everywhere. Desk drawers were left open or dumped. Books had been yanked off shelves and discarded on the floor, couch cushions jettisoned.

"Someone tossed the place," I said.

The slide show continued, showing a similar mess in a bedroom, living area, and kitchen.

"That's the way it looks to me," Gord said.

"Was it a robbery?"

"If so, they forgot to take the valuables."

"That kind of rules out suicide," I said.

"Possibly," Greenleaf said.

"Possibly? C'mon, Gord. The guy's found dead, and his place is tossed? What else could it be?"

"Two separate incidents," he said. "Or a sign that the judge wasn't stable during his final hours. Who knows?"

"You don't believe that."

"No, Vince, I don't."

"What's the nephew say?"

"That's the thing: Peter Sorenson's not saying much. In fact, he seemed confused about the condition of the house."

"Confused?"

"Like he didn't know. Wouldn't you call the police if you came home and found it looking like this?" Gord said, and he gestured at the screen.

"He didn't?"

"Claims he was out at a bar late and that he came home plastered and went straight to bed, so he didn't notice anything unusual."

"Must have really been out of it."

"Yeah, but the funny thing is, he wasn't home when the housekeeper arrived yesterday morning. She flipped out and called us. He came strolling in about a half hour after I got there from Explorer's Park. When I asked him where he'd been, he claimed he'd been out for an early breakfast, but— get this—he couldn't name the restaurant. An early-bird breakfast isn't the usual behavior you'd expect from someone with a major hangover. And even a major hangover doesn't explain how he missed the mess on his way out."

"You think he knew the house was trashed? Or maybe he was the one who did it? Maybe he was searching for something?"

"If he did, he's a phenomenal actor," Gord said. "He seemed genuinely worked up once he realized someone had been through the house. And he didn't relax until he'd looked around the judge's office and made sure nothing valuable was taken."

"How'd he react when you told him about his uncle's death?"

"I'd say he was bewildered, kind of like he was caught off guard."

"Was he still drunk?"

"No. But I'm pretty sure he was lying about something. My guess is that he probably didn't make it home the previous night."

I sipped Gord's bitter coffee, winced, and put the foam cup

on his desk, wondering how I'd tolerated the stuff for the last few years.

"Did you find any more X-rated stuff like the photo pinned on the judge?"

"A couple of DVDs, some photos printed off a Web site."

"You think the judge was really a perv?"

"What I think doesn't matter. What I know is that the judge didn't have a DVD player—unless it was stolen. Ditto a computer or printer, and his housekeeper is adamant he had no interest in the stuff. In fact, I doubt anyone from your office will be welcome around there for a while—she was livid about the *Chronicle* story yesterday."

"Someone planted the porn?"

Gord shrugged.

"And nothing was stolen?"

"Nothing of value, according to the nephew and the housekeeper. But . . ."

"But what?"

"Patrice Berklee called me after she heard about the judge's death," Gord said. "The judge had spent a lot of time at the historical society recently, and he'd taken copious notes—"

"And you couldn't find those notes," I said.

"No, we couldn't. Nor could we find historical documents she said he owned—journals of some sort kept by his ancestors. Patrice came out to his house last night to help me search it again, in case I'd overlooked something she might recognize. We found nothing pertaining to his research."

"Which was?"

"Early Apostle Bay history and property records. Apparently he was searching for some kind of document or contract."

I grabbed the cup, took another rancid sip, and glanced at the slide show again.

"Why?"

"According to Patrice, Judge Sorenson believed he had a line on something that would stop the development at Explorer's Park."

Chapter Fifteen

I sat up so fast, I sloshed coffee onto Gord's desk. He held up a hand, warning me to back down.

"Stop the development?"

"Don't jump—"

"But that means Jack Reynolds had a motive. It makes him the most likely suspect."

"Not so fast, Vince. First of all, we don't know if there is a document, or if it would really stop or delay the project. It hardly seems likely that someone would kill the judge for a piece of paper that's only rumored to exist."

"Yeah, but what if—"

"Second, Reynolds has an indisputable alibi. Give me some credit. It's the first thing I checked after talking with Patrice. The ME estimates the time of death sometime between midnight and three. Several people, including two council members, were with Jack at his house during that time."

"He had visitors until three in the morning?"

"A poker game. They didn't wrap up until three-thirty."

"That's convenient," I said. "Who are the other witnesses? His business partner? The developer?"

Gord shrugged and leaned back in his chair. I grabbed a paper towel from near his coffeepot and wiped the spill from his desk.

"So what's in this document?" I asked.

"It's all speculation, Vince. Why don't you talk to Patrice?"

I looked at the door, now regretting that I'd let him close it. I could have learned all this from Patrice when I visited her later that morning and put together a great story. Gord seemed to read my mind.

"What's the big deal? I thought you weren't covering this."

"Yeah, but . . ."

"You can't let go of anything, can you?" He sounded disappointed.

"But this puts a whole different light on what happened."

"Not really," he said. "We don't know anything. What if, for example, the judge did find some hidden document, but it was the opposite of what he thought—it supported the city council's decision? Could he have been distraught enough to kill himself?"

"Right. He trashed his house, killed himself, and left behind evidence that he was a pervert because he wasn't thinking clearly. Get real, Gord. The judge was murdered."

"Probably. I'm just saying, let us investigate before you leap to conclusions."

"Like concluding Monty Haver's a suspect?" I stood and moved to the door. I didn't want any more information off the record.

"Sit back down a minute," he said.

"I don't think so, Gord."

"Please. There's more I think you should hear."

"I think so too," I said, pulling open the door. "I just don't want the information with strings attached."

I stepped from Greenleaf's office and nearly crashed into Ashley Adams and Archie Freeman. They both glared at me.

"Good morning," I said. To Freeman I added, "How goes the investigation?"

"I'm sure your buddy told you everything."

"He told me that the Lions are looking at another losing season."

Freeman pushed past me and went into his office. I cut in front of Ashley, pulled out my recorder, and followed him.

"Detective, how does the judge's death affect your campaign?"

"Get the—" Speed Demon noticed the recorder and held his tongue.

I knew I was being stupid, taking out the frustration I'd felt in Gord's office, but I couldn't seem to help myself.

He said through clenched teeth, "What kind of a question is that?"

"Do you think it's appropriate for you to investigate his death, considering that you were his political opponent?"

"You little—" Freeman came around his desk at me.

"Vince!" The deep bass voice startled me, and I juggled the recorder. I turned, almost bumping into Ashley, and saw the chief's broad frame filling the doorway.

"In my office," he said, jerking his thumb like an umpire. "Now!"

No one who saw his glare could accuse me of getting special treatment from my father's best friend.

I pocketed the recorder, took a final glance at Freeman, who didn't seem mollified by the chief's intervention, and then walked into the corridor. The chief waved me past, and I heard him say, "You too, young lady," and then I heard Ashley's heels striking the linoleum as she followed me.

I stepped into the chief's spartan office and dropped into one of the two straight-backed chairs in front of his desk. I heard him enter and tell Ashley to have a seat too.

"I'll stand," she said.

"Suit yourself," he said. He moved behind his green metal desk, the same one he'd had when my dad brought me to visit here as a child. I was sure of it because my name, written with permanent marker on a far leg when I was much smaller, was still there—I'd checked. He wore his standard plainclothes uniform of khaki dress pants, white button-down shirt, and dark tie. He remained standing too.

I watched him and Ashley glare at each other and wasn't sure if I should rise also, kind of even things out, or if I should stay down, below the line of fire. A plate of cookies on the chief's desk—completely out of place for his office, as he'd never allowed food there before—caught my attention. I leaned forward and grabbed the plate, thinking it seemed somewhat familiar.

"C'mon, you guys," I said. "Have a seat. Let's all have a cookie."

They ignored me. The chief had clamped his lips shut; the tendons in his neck were taut to the point of stretching his collar. Ashley seemed a little unsure but determined to win whatever this contest of wills was about. I took a cookie—they were oatmeal raisin—and returned the platter to the chief's desk.

The chief broke eye contact first and turned to me. "I am the contact for all media inquiries," he said. "My detectives have a job to do, and they can't do it when you're bothering them."

"You can't—" Ashley started.

"I can. In fact, this office is supposed to be a secure area. The public, meaning you two, are not allowed to wander the halls as if you owned the place. From now on, if you wish to see me, you will wait outside the security glass until an officer is available to escort you to my office."

"C'mon, Chief."

"You have only yourself to blame, Vince. Your freedom here was a privilege, and you of all people have crossed the line too many times."

This was too weird. I'd been roaming these offices since I was a child, since before there was a security door and bulletproof glass at the entrance.

"I don't see why I should be punished if he's the problem," Ashley said to the chief.

"He's not the only problem, young lady," the chief said. "Your behavior at a crime scene yesterday was not just irresponsible, it was criminal."

Ashley started to protest, but the chief cut her off again.

"You lied to my officer about discovering the judge. That's a two-year misdemeanor called obstruction of justice. I don't see how we could trust you in any regard."

I thought she'd deny it. Instead she countered, "This is a public facility. We have the right to be here."

The chief smiled and relaxed a little. "No. You don't."

"But—" Ashley was the one turning red now.

I knew better than to argue. The chief had a history of saying things like this and, over time, backing off. And it only affected my morning coffee and conversation with Greenleaf, which, now that I had Glory several mornings a week, was happening at the Whitefish Cafe anyway.

"What about seeing the overnight dispatch log?" she asked. "How can we do that from out in the hall?"

"I ought to make you F-O-I-A it," the chief said, referring to the Freedom of Information Act. He held up his hands, anticipating our complaints, paused, and then said, "I'll have the dispatcher print an extra copy of the overnight activity—which I'll review—and you can pick it up at the front window each morning."

Ashley had her PDA out now and was scribbling something with the stylus. I thought about asking the chief the same question I'd tried on Freeman: was there a conflict of interest regarding Freeman's investigating the judge's death? I decided I'd save it for later, when he'd calmed down. Instead I asked, "Who made the cookies?"

He seemed surprised by the question, even a little embarrassed. "Your mother," he answered.

"Huh?" Mom didn't bake. She was an outdoors, work-in-the-garden, snowblow-the-driveway type of person. If I needed a snack for school, or when I had a birthday party, Mom bought the cookies or cake at the store. "What did you do to rate that?"

He ignored me, so I grabbed another cookie and took a bite. Ashley looked up from her PDA at me with obvious annoyance.

"If I could interrupt this homey little conversation, I'd like to know, Chief, why you called it a crime scene. Does that indicate you're investigating the judge's death as a homicide?" she demanded.

That erased the chief's embarrassed look. "Who said it was a homicide?"

"I heard you found other evidence of pornography at the judge's home. What can you tell me about that?" she pressed.

"Who told you that?"

"A source."

"Tell me who," the chief demanded.

"Was this a suicide or a homicide?" she asked.

"We are currently investigating the judge's death," the chief said. "I'll let you know when we have more information that we can release publicly."

"Surely, Chief Weathers—"

The chief's intercom beeped, and Gail's voice blurted, "Chief, Mayor Reynolds just called. He said he and a Mr. Peter Sorenson are waiting for you up in the mayor's office."

"The judge's nephew?" I asked.

The chief ignored me and grumbled something under his breath. Then he pushed his intercom button. "Tell him I'll be right up, Gail. And please send an officer back to escort out my guests."

"If you'll excuse me," the chief said, coming around from behind his desk. "I have more pressing problems than babysitting you two."

"You can't—" Ashley started.

"Thanks for the cookies, Chief," I said. Then, standing to leave, I added, "You should try one, Ashley. They're quite tasty."

Chapter Sixteen

Two steps outside city hall Ashley turned on me. "You did that on purpose," she said.

"What?" I said, putting up my hands in self-defense.

"Getting into Detective Freeman's face so he'd get mad and quit helping me. Getting me kicked out of there. Does it make you feel good? Sabotaging my story?"

"Get real, Ashley. Your antics yesterday are what got us kicked out. That's why the chief almost popped a vein in his forehead."

"I got the story," she said, pointing her stylus at me. "I got the story while you got stuck there. And now you're angry that it's my story and that I've worked a source inside the department you could never get."

"Freeman hates the press. There's no way he'd be a source."

"Way," she said. "He's angry because the chief won't let him investigate this case."

"Smart move by the chief," I said. "But don't trust Speed Demon Freeman. He has his own agenda."

"Oh, and I should trust you?"

"Yes. I told you about Monty Haver, didn't I?"

She flashed me her disbelieving smirk, and for a moment I felt sorry for her, and I wondered if she'd carried a chip on her shoulder all through college too.

"I know you think I'm jealous," I said. "But I'm not. As foreign as this concept is, I'm watching out for the *Chronicle.* I work there too. And I'll still be living in Apostle Bay long after you move on to your next assignment."

"I see. Then if that's the case, why were you here this morning—I mean, besides watching out for the newspaper's interest, of course?"

"Shootin' the breeze with Gordon Greenleaf."

"About what?"

"Stuff."

"Yeah, stuff having to do with Judge Sorenson's death, I'm sure. Since Detective Greenleaf won't seem to come clean with me, why don't you give me an update?"

"I . . . uh . . ."

"I see. The good ol' boys network."

"It's not that—"

"Forget it, Vince. Just forget it."

Chapter Seventeen

Ashley took off—I assumed toward her car, since she wasn't heading in the direction of the *Chronicle*. I grabbed the sweet roll leftovers from my Bronco and then walked diagonally across the parking lot and downtown park to the newspaper office.

The newsroom was empty except for Gina Holt, who was banging her keyboard and chomping her nicotine gum. She greeted me without looking up.

"Where's the boss?" I asked. I was a bit surprised that Lou wasn't sunbathing in his monitor's glare, giving the wire stories a last review before our editorial meeting.

"He's down in the pressroom," she said. "Changing some part."

"Again, huh? Anyone I know die?" I asked, nodding toward the obits on her desk.

"You were dying yesterday, boy. At the hands of Little Miss Go-getter. How'd that feel?"

"Don't remind me."

"You know my motto, Vince. You only get stepped on—"

"I know, I know, when you act like a doormat. Thanks, Gina."

I dropped onto my desk chair, then noticed one of Lou's molar-mashed No. 2s and a stained mug next to my keyboard. On my monitor hung a sticky note, on which Lou'd scrawled: *$ damages???* Behind that was an edited version of my cemetery vandalism story. Lou had left the length intact.

I called Aristotle, glad that he lived where he worked so he was easy to reach this early. He pulled a figure of five to ten thousand bucks out of the air as a damage estimate. I added it to the copy, thinking I must be slipping. Normally I wouldn't need a reminder from Lou to include a fact like that.

Lou came into the bull pen as I was saving the file. Black grease stained his shirt, and he was wiping his hands with a rag when he stopped by my desk to retrieve his mug.

"Glad to see you could make it in today," he said. His sarcasm lacked its usual edge, and there seemed to be more red than white in his eyes this morning. "You see my note?"

"Already took care of it," I said. "Working on the press again?"

"Had to repack the bearings on a roller before today's run. It took a bit longer than we thought."

Since coming out of retirement and buying the *Chronicle* at a bankruptcy auction almost three years ago, Lou'd been rebuilding our ancient press piece by piece. Or, to be more accurate, Lou was assisting John Reigle, our blacksmithing farm mechanic turned press foreman, in his effort to rebuild the obsolete beast, a job that required Reigle to make some of the replacement parts in the forge in his barn. At first the work had revived Lou, but lately I think the stress and lack of sleep was catching up with him. He'd been crankier than usual, and the humor that used to lurk behind his criticism and make it tolerable had disappeared. I hoped he wasn't heading toward another deadline heart failure.

Lou tossed the rag into my trash, grabbed his mug and pencil, and went to the community coffeepot for a refill. Mort Maki passed him on his way in, grunted a hello as he tossed his canvas briefcase onto the desk across from me, and, following his standard morning ritual, headed toward the lunchroom with a brown paper bag. I'd lifted the doggie bag to hand him, but he was in such a hurry, he missed my offer.

"Who's going to replace the judge?" Lou asked as he walked over to his workstation.

"It's up to the governor," I said. "But she might let it ride, since a new judge will be elected in two months. If that's the case, a visiting judge from a different county can hear cases."

"Is the story done?"

"Just about. I need to confirm a few details with the clerk. I'll have it for you as soon as their office opens."

Lou grunted and started scanning his monitor. He said, without looking my way, "How long do you plan to grace us with your presence this morning?"

"After deadline I want to chase down a few leads. And don't forget, I'm off tomorrow."

"Right," he said, forcing the word out past the pencil clenched in his jaw. Still scanning his screen, he asked, "Leads on what?"

"Just some coincidences regarding the grave desecration, the Explorer's Park development, and the judge's death. I've got a hunch they're all tied together some way."

"I told you to give whatever you have on that to Ashley. She's covering the story. Let her do the chasing."

"I have. I mean, I will. I mean . . . listen, Lou. I don't really have enough info to give her. At least nothing that makes sense yet. It's just a bunch of weird loose ends that have me curious."

I watched him click his mouse, probably dragging a story off the wire, and then sip his coffee. He still didn't look my way.

"If the tables were turned, would you want her to tell you?"

"Sure, but—"

"Give her what you have, and let her do the work."

"I will, Lou. As soon as I figure out if there's anything to it."

"I don't think you're listening to me," he said, this time turning his bloodshot eyes on me. "I want someone who's gonna work this story full-time, not pick it up and drop it from day to day. Give her what you've got—even your hunches—and let her do the digging, especially since you're not going to be here tomorrow. Am I clear?"

"Yeah, but—"

"Good. I'm glad we're of the same mind. Speaking of Ashley, where is she?"

"I saw her—"

"I'm here," she said, stepping into the room, waving her PDA. Her face was flushed, as if she'd been jogging. "I've got some good stuff."

Maki, on his way back to his desk, quipped, "Then let's go out back and smoke it."

She ignored him and walked to Lou's desk. "I just got off the phone with the judge's housekeeper. She confirmed that the police discovered more porn when they searched his house yesterday."

"It's a plant," I said.

"That's what she says. But . . . Hey!" She turned toward me. "Is that what Detective Greenleaf told you this morning?"

I shrugged and wished I'd kept my mouth shut.

"Ah, this is getting good," Maki said. He lifted his stork legs up onto his desk and leaned back.

"What Greenleaf told me is that the judge's housekeeper wanted a piece of your hide yesterday. How'd you get her to talk for an interview?" I asked.

"It wasn't that hard."

"Did you tell her who you were?"

"She knew I was a reporter," Ashley said. "That's all that matters."

Maki leaned toward me and whispered, "Probably said she was Lucy DeMott. Everybody wants to talk to the TV queen."

I guessed Maki was right. Let Lou worry about it, I thought.

Ashley was looking at the boss again and explaining that she had corroboration on the porn found in the judge's house.

"Peter Sorenson confirmed it," she said, and I swear I could hear a self-satisfied smile in her tone. "He told me that someone was going to break the news soon, so he thinks the judge was forced into suicide."

"Oh, c'mon," I said. "It wasn't a suicide. You're heading so far in the wrong direction on this, it's amazing."

"Maybe if she had all the information, she wouldn't be," Lou said. "Right after our meeting Vince is going to give you everything he has, Ashley. *Everything.*"

"I don't need his help."

"Oh, grow up!" Lou shouted. He slammed his mug down, shattering it. The room went silent except for the hum of computers, the morning news babble playing on the wall TV behind him, and the coffee dripping off his desk onto the age-old vinyl tile below. "Vince has a ton more resources than you because he knows everyone in town. I hired you because of your brain, not your pride. If you want to excel in this business, start using it."

He stunned us all with the outburst. Ashley went scarlet and walked out of the room. Maki pulled his legs off his desk and sat upright, as if he was in an old-time Catholic school and the nun had just whacked his shins with her ruler. I kept thinking I should feel satisfaction at Lou's comments, but instead I felt like a jerk.

Lou broke the silence. "Let's go over what we've got for deadline. Ashley's got follow-up on the judge's death with art. Vince has the sidebar on who replaces the judge, and also art and copy on the cemetery vandalism. Maki's got an update on the development with the proposed zoning change and construction schedule. What else do we have for local news?"

No one wanted to be the first to speak. Ashley returned to her desk and sat, not looking at anyone. I think we were all watching her in our peripheral vision.

"Well?" Lou asked. "Anything? How about the future of the Sorenson Foundation, Ashley? Did you pin down the nephew yet?"

"He's still distraught over the death of his uncle—"

I couldn't help snorting at that.

"—and told me he isn't ready to think about that yet."

"Okay, then, let's—"

"How about tonight's vigil for the judge?" I suggested.

Lou gave me a blank look. I glanced over at Mort.

"I'm not doing anything with that," he said.

"What is it?" Lou asked.

"His wife," Maki said, waving a hand in my direction, "is trying to capitalize on the judge's death and get some free publicity."

"Mort, that's a crock—"

"I almost choked when she called me about it last night," he said.

I slid the bag of sweet rolls over to the edge of my desk and nudged it into the trash can.

"I have it in my story," Ashley said.

"Huh?" both Maki and I said in unison.

"I've got it covered," she said. "The Superior Citizens Against Lakeshore Development is sponsoring a candlelight vigil tonight at Explorer's Park in memory of the judge. I planned to cover the event too, since I heard Peter Sorenson is going to attend."

Maki glared at me, obviously thinking I'd engineered this.

I shrugged. His loss, I thought.

"At least we have it," Lou said, shaking his head. "You've got about thirty minutes to clean up your stories and take care of the questions I left. Get to work."

Lou ignored the puddle on his desk and floor, or maybe left it there as a reminder to us, and went back to working on the inside pages. I rolled my chair over to Ashley's desk.

"Have you had a chance to call Monty Haver?" I asked.

She didn't answer, just scowled at her monitor.

"I've got to call him for my piece anyway, and I know the police questioned him yesterday. How about I see if I can get anything from him about the judge's death, and you can work it into your story?"

"Whatever," she said.

"Okay, here's what I know about the porn, Ashley. But I don't have it from a source we can use."

"Greenleaf—"

"It doesn't matter who. The stuff was likely planted by someone; it's not the judge's."

"That's the most ridiculous—"

"Why would a guy own X-rated DVDs and not have a DVD player?"

"So what are you saying? I should pull it from my story?"

I shrugged. "It's up to you. But I think you're being played. It seems odd to me that Peter Sorenson would share that info with you and smear his dead uncle. The cops don't trust Peter. I don't think you should either."

"Why don't they trust him?" she asked.

"Just a hunch that something's not quite right," I said.

Ashley seemed to consider this a moment; then she said, "I think you're the one trying to play me. If I drop what I have, there's nothing left to today's story."

"Not true. You've got the judge's background, you've got the vigil, you've got comments from the community—you probably have more than Lou can fit on the front page anyway, and hardly anybody reads the jump."

She didn't look pleased.

"Why don't you try two things? First, I don't know how you got the housekeeper talking, but try to work your magic again and ask her about the judge's house being searched. Someone trashed the place—either vandalism, or, more likely, they were looking for something."

"She told me that."

"Okay. Then take what you have from her and from the nephew, and call the chief—tell him what you've got and what you're running with. Make a bargain."

"But he'll—"

"He'll yell at you and moan and groan, but he'll give you

something you can use. And he won't steer you the wrong way. That's one thing you can count on with the chief."

"I don't believe you," she said.

"Fine, do it your way. I'm just trying to tell you that this is going to be a much bigger story than an old guy looking at dirty pictures. You're going to look foolish when the real story comes out because you had no patience."

"Oh, really?" she said. "From what I hear, patience isn't your strong suit either."

"But looking foolish has been. Maybe I've learned a tiny bit about how to avoid it."

Ashley opened her mouth to retort, but no words came out. She looked down and fiddled with her PDA a moment, then, without looking up, asked, "What do you suggest?"

"Let me chase a few ideas after deadline and get back with you. I'll give you something you can sink your teeth into."

"Oh, I'm supposed to sit here like a good little girl and wait for you to do my work for me?"

I felt like telling her that was exactly what she ought to do, but instead I took a deep breath and tried to sound accommodating.

"No. Please, just give me an hour, and I'll call you with some leads. I just don't want to send you on a wild goose chase if I'm wrong."

"Where are you going?" she asked.

"To check some files at the courthouse, and then to confirm something with Patrice Berklee over at the historical society museum."

"Why can't I do it?"

"Jeez, Ashley, just give me an hour after deadline, and I'll call you. Work on some briefs, or grab some lunch or something."

She seemed to debate this, then looked at her watch. "An hour?"

"Yes."

"You're going to the courthouse first, then the historical society?"

"Yes!"

"Okay," she said. "Call me on my cell when you leave the courthouse."

"Sure," I said. "Whatever."

I rolled back to my desk, noticing on the way that my trash can was now empty. I looked over at Maki. He stuffed a hunk of sweet roll into his mouth and winked at me.

Chapter Eighteen

After deadline I walked the three blocks from our office to the Superior County Courthouse. I hoped for better luck connecting with Haver there, since he'd refused to take my calls that morning. Rhonda had helped me flesh out the story on deadline and tried to pump me for more gossip on the judge. She'd whispered that she had more news to share about Monty's "situation" when I arrived.

It's an uphill walk to the courthouse, on a grade steep enough to get my heart pounding and stretch my calves. The imposing brown sandstone structure sits on the highest point in Apostle Bay.

The building is topped with a large, circular clerestory visible from anywhere in town and from several miles out on the lake. It's designed to look like a lighthouse, and when the morning and evening sun reflects off the glass at a low angle, one might even think the structure had a signal beacon.

It doesn't. Instead, the windows allow natural light into the courthouse atrium. I passed through there on my way to the clerk's office, glancing up at the portraits of all the circuit judges who had served Superior County and wondering where they'd place Judge Sorenson's.

At the end of the southern wing I opened the opaque glass door and greeted Rhonda, who stood behind the counter tapping on a keyboard. Pale as a nocturnal creature and dressed in her standard buttoned-to-the-neck cardigan, ankle-length skirt, and clogs, Rhonda came around the clerk's counter to greet me. She took my arm and guided me to a wooden bench outside the document room. The bench, like the surrounding walls, was dark, polished wood that seemed to absorb the office's cold fluorescent light and reflect it back in a softer hue. She leaned close and grilled me about my discovery of the judge's body. I started to explain, but she interrupted.

"That stuff about the judge being a pervert is pure bunk," she said.

"I agree."

As if she didn't hear me, she continued. "It's such a joke. The judge couldn't use a computer to save his life. He did everything the old way: took notes longhand, wrote his opinions on legal pads in pencil—not even a mechanical pencil mind you, number two's, the kind you have to sharpen. We had to type everything for him. I guarantee he wasn't surfing the Internet, looking at triple-X sites, because he just didn't know how."

"He didn't use the Internet?"

"Ha! The last time the judge's computer was turned on before yesterday was almost a year ago, and that was for some kind of system upgrade. I got that straight from the tech guy. He was in there with the cops."

"Which cops? Detective Greenleaf?"

"Yeah, the good-looking one. And the bailiff—he was there basically to make sure the police didn't mess things up too much."

"What did they find?"

"Well," she said, drawing out the word and looking around the empty office as if she needed to make sure no one was listening. "The first thing they found was Monty. Walked right in on him. They keyed the door, and there he was, sitting behind the judge's desk, going through his drawers. The bailiff gave me the scoop."

"Monty? What was he looking for?"

"He told them he was searching for a court file he needed."

"But . . . Didn't you tell me yesterday that you handled all the work with the judge?"

"Very good," she said. She tilted her head toward Haver's closed door. "The chief's in there with him now," she said.

"I see. Did Monty find anything?"

"He said no. They kicked him out and started their own search. But they don't believe him."

An explosion of voices behind Monty's office door interrupted her. I could tell Rhonda was itching to drift that way and eavesdrop.

"That's why the chief's here," she said. "I guess they were looking for a particular item in the judge's office, and it didn't turn it up. They even tore into some walls and worked a few floorboards loose, looking for a hiding spot. They think Monty might have whatever it is, or maybe he knows where it is. But, like I said, if they're looking for X-rated pictures, they're barking up the wrong tree."

I'd take a pretty good guess they were looking for the judge's missing notes, but I didn't think now was the right time for Rhonda to share that info with half the town.

"Did Monty tell you what case file he was looking for?"

"He won't talk about it, but I can assure you he wasn't looking for a case file."

"What, then?"

She shrugged her thin shoulders. "Vince," she said, "I think they're going to arrest Monty."

"C'mon."

"No, really. The cops have been asking everyone about that big blowup last week. The one between Monty and the judge. And it was a big one. I thought Monty was going to have a stroke he was so hot. And there's more." She dropped her voice so low, I had to hold my breath to hear. "Someone saw his car parked at the judge's house the night he died."

I wondered if that was what Greenleaf had been planning to share before I stormed out of his office.

"Yesterday you told me there's always been bad blood between Monty and the judge. What's that all about?"

"Who knows?" she said. "Something that goes way back. Monty wouldn't ever tell me when I asked, but I think it had something to do with their families, and, you know"—she bent closer—"Monty's great-great-grandfather killed himself, and it was *just* like the judge. He hanged himself from a tree down by the lake. Now isn't that too weird?"

"It's definitely weird," I said.

"Monty's innocent," she said, placing a hand on my arm. "Do you think you can help him?"

"Me? How could I help?"

"You figured things out last year—you know, when there were those problems with your mom and your wife."

"I got lucky. You know that. Besides, that whole thing hinged on the information you and Monty gave me."

Rhonda smiled and sat up a little straighter. Both she and

Monty had reveled in the part they'd played solving that mystery.

"What do you think we should do?" she asked.

"Sarah Dodge told me I should start by checking the domestic violence cases the judge heard."

I saw Rhonda's eyes light up, and she practically leaped from the bench. "Of course," she said. "Reggie Novak. Bingo! I should have thought of that."

She walked through the swinging gate and behind the counter to a terminal.

"Reggie Novak?"

Rhonda typed a few keystrokes, studied the screen, and came back around the counter.

"C'mon," she said, grabbing my upper arm and pulling me into the document room. She went to a wall of file cabinets, ran her finger over the labels, and stopped on a drawer. She opened it and plucked out a file.

"Reggie Novak," she said. "He's Elaine's ex."

"Elaine?"

"You know. I can't believe I didn't think of this before. Elaine does the cleaning in here."

I vaguely remembered a slight woman with blond hair and glasses who always seemed to be floating around in the background when I came to look up a file. "The lady who's always polishing the wood?"

"That's her. Elaine Novak."

She led me back out to the counter and opened the file.

"Her ex, Reggie, beat her up pretty good a few years back, and the judge nailed him with the maximum sentence. Then the judge got her the custodial job here, to try to help her get back on her feet. I was court clerk at the sentencing, and Reggie—let me tell you, he was a real piece of work—went berserk. I thought he was coming over me to get at the judge before the bailiff and his lawyer wrestled him down."

I flipped through the file, not really sure what she wanted me to see.

"You think he could've killed the judge?"

"Oh, yeah," she said. "No doubt. I'd have you talk to Elaine, but she didn't come in today. I figured it was because she was broken up about the judge's death—the judge treated her real well, you know. Besides getting her the job here, he was paying her on the side for some secretarial work, some genealogy research he was doing. She was typing all his notes into a laptop. Oh, goodness, you don't think Reggie went after her too, do you?"

"I—"

Haver's office door flew open, and the chief stormed out, almost barreling over me as he came through the counter's hinged section. Behind him I saw Haver, his face purple with rage.

At the same moment the outer door to the clerk's office opened, and I turned to see Freeman stepping in. Both he and the chief looked surprised to see each other.

I backed away from the counter, out of the firing line.

"Detective Freeman, I thought we discussed that you're steering clear of here," the chief said.

"You mean you've cut me out because I ruffled too many feathers in this town?"

With what I considered to be amazing control, knowing his propensity to freak out when his authority was questioned, the chief said, "I think it would be best if we spoke about this back at the office."

"What, so you can have your little favorite, Greenleaf—"

"Detective Freeman—"

"—pussyfoot around so that no one's sensibilities are upset—"

"Detective Freeman—"

"—while we overlook the fact that our upstanding judge was a—"

"Archie, *shut up!*" the chief boomed. When the echo died, he added, "That's an order."

Freeman didn't waver, and I thought for a moment he might refuse, but instead he said, "Yes, sir." He handed Rhonda an envelope, then turned and walked out the door.

I saw Haver close his office door and heard the lock click home.

The chief sighed, nodded toward me, and said, "Vince."

It was a greeting, nothing more, but it sounded an awful lot like, "What did I do to deserve this?"

"Hi again, Chief."

Rhonda, meanwhile, opened the envelope.

"Just a form he needed to file for November's election," she said.

Chapter Nineteen

I didn't know what had happened in Monty's office, but the man wasn't talking. Indeed, he wouldn't open his door or answer his intercom after the chief left. Rhonda and I tried for a minute or two, and then I told Rhonda I'd call her later and booked out of the office, hoping to catch the chief. I wanted to pump him for information about Monty and tell him about Elaine Novak.

Instead, when I jogged down the hall and into the court-house's rotunda, I found myself in the middle of a one-man, one-medium news conference.

Rudy Clark, our county prosecutor, is a small man with a supersize ego and a politician's ability to sound intelligent even when he's blathering. He stood tall in his platform shoes, holding a mic and smiling into the bright halogen lamp shining off Lucy DeMott's camera. Clark wore his courtroom suit, complete with red power tie, and spoke with a somber dignity that came across, to my admittedly biased view, as calculated and fake.

DeMott, looking every bit the part of the professional anchorwoman she'd one day be—pressed, dark-blue skirt and blazer, every hair in place, her body far too skinny to be healthy—stood next to her tripod, scratching notes. I wondered if she had any interest in Clark's speech or was thinking about her imminent departure from our little town.

The good television journalists live out their two-year contracts in this remote outpost, picking up enough video to make an effective demo tape, and then they move to larger markets, where they not only have their own cameraperson lugging the equipment for them, but also get more exposure. Lucy, I know, is near the end of her sentence, and I'm not sure whether I'll miss her work or be glad for the competition's loss.

". . . a great tragedy for our community," Clark said. "I can only hope my years of experience enforcing the laws of this community and my success at keeping criminals off our streets will help me continue the man's fine work."

Give me a break. Clark was announcing his candidacy for judge.

"Write-in campaigns are rarely successful, Mr. Clark," DeMott said. "What makes you think you'll be able to win?"

"Because, Lucy, many friends and citizens have approached me and said they hoped someone with my experience and knowledge of the law would be willing to step in under these circumstances—with the untimely death of the judge, that is. So I think the campaign will be a real grassroots effort, something driven by the people of this community who see the need for a qualified candidate."

A race between this joker and Freeman? I'm not sure who'd be worse. No, that's not true. At least Clark is such a politician, he wouldn't do anything that might cost him votes, and he did know and enforce the law. I had to give him that. Freeman, on the other hand, was a cluster bomb with a loose wire.

We definitely needed to talk Sarah Dodge into running.

DeMott flicked off the spotlight. She stepped forward to take the mic and shook Clark's hand.

"Sorry I'm late for the press conference," I said.

DeMott turned and smiled, happy in the knowledge that it was past my deadline, so it was her story to break.

"Hi, Vince," she said, winding her cable and taking down her equipment.

Normally Clark would be avoiding me like the plague. His media interviews are well planned and happen on his terms. But I guess he needed me now, so he stuck his hand toward me and forced a smile. We shook.

"So, you're announcing a write-in campaign for judge?"

"Well, many citizens have approached me. . . ."

"Yeah," I said, not bothering to open my notebook. He noticed and trailed off. "How about I walk you back to your office, and you can tell me all about it?"

I saw from the look in Lucy's eyes that she knew I was trying to get him away from her to ask about something else, and she was debating whether it was worth following us or continuing to pack her equipment. I decided for her.

"Talk to you later, Lucy," I said.

I guided Clark down the corridor. He began to blab about his years of experience and the reasons he'd reluctantly decided to join the race. I kept nodding and "uh-huh"-ing until we made it to his office. Then I asked, "Why do you think Judge Sorenson was killed?"

"Save your breath, Vince," he said, his smile now replaced by the look of disdain he always reserved for me. "I'll only answer questions about my decision to run for judge."

"Did you know that Monty Haver's a suspect in the judge's death?"

"I guess you didn't hear me," Clark said.

"Okay, how about: do you think your opponent, Detective Archie Freeman, would make a good judge?"

"I can only speak to my own experience, not his lack thereof." Clark smiled again, as if he'd made a little joke. "You'll have to excuse me," he said, checking his watch. "I'm late for a meeting."

Chapter Twenty

My car was at city hall. I needed to pick it up, swing by the historical society, and then get Glory, and I had about forty-five minutes to do it. On my way down the hill I tried both the chief and Gordon on my cell, but Gail told me they were out. I left a message for Gord.

I bagged the idea of checking in with Ashley. I wouldn't have time to talk with Patrice and pick up Glory if I got tied up arguing with her again.

The Apostle Bay Historical Society is housed in a former bank building, a limestone structure with gilt-painted revolving doors, storefront windows, and a monstrous bronze canopy hanging over the main entrance. As I drove past, heading toward the alley behind the building where I liked to park, I thought I glimpsed Ashley coming out the revolving door.

Just like her, I thought. She couldn't wait for me and didn't even know the right questions to ask. And Patrice doesn't take to well to pushy people. I'd learned to play by her rules, something you needed to do if you wanted her help.

I parked in a loading zone and entered through the building's rear door, climbing the staircase to the main exhibit floor. The society's current exhibit on the timber industry, heavy on photos and dioramas, filled the space where tellers and loan officers once counted money. Local volunteers had constructed a scale model of an old-time logging operation in the exhibit area's center. The model featured a forest, logging camp, and a pond and millrace with water circulating via a hidden pump, which showed how logs were transported downstream.

I made a mental note to bring Glory back to see it as I passed through a gate of twisted wrought iron, the first line of defense for the old bank vault. I entered the research library. At the back end of the library was the former vault, a two-story structure with a massive circular door, that now held the county's most vital historical documents and photos.

I'd once been allowed to enter the vault, Patrice Berklee's inner sanctum, and felt privileged, knowing I was one of the few. When I reached the entrance, I could hear her in the lower level slamming a drawer closed.

I leaned into the vault, over the alarm sensor that would beep if I crossed the line, and called down. "Patrice? It's Vince. Do you have a minute?"

She called back up, "Well, that was quick."

There was a moment of silence, some rustling, and then I heard her clanging on the circular metal stair. Halfway up the spiral she came into view, dressed as usual in her raven-like black-on-black outfit. She looked peeved as she peeled off her protective cotton gloves, and I hoped Ashley hadn't put her into an uncooperative mood.

"You missed a good class last night at the pool," I said.

"You need to teach that girl some manners," she replied.

"Glory?" I said, hoping to derail her from a lecture.

"No, that girl you sent in here to talk with me. She was so rude, I asked her to leave."

"Oh. Ashley."

"Yes. The rules here are simple. You need to—"

"Hold on, Patrice," I interrupted. "I didn't send her."

"Well, she said you sent her. She told me that she was taking over your duties, and I'd be dealing with her now. Then she demanded I tell her what I was going to tell you. I told her that boorish people get what they deserve around here: nothing."

At this she folded her arms and, had she been Glory's age, probably would have stamped her foot.

"I'm sorry, Patrice. But don't blame me; she learned those manners at your former institution. We hired her right out of MSU."

Patrice glared, and I realized it had been a faux pas to blame Michigan State, even as a joke.

"I have friends who teach in the journalism program, and I can assure you, she didn't learn that behavior at State," Patrice said.

I got the feeling this was heading in the wrong direction and tried to think of a way to get Patrice back on topic when a thought crossed my mind.

"You have friends there still?"

"Of course."

"If you get a chance, would you mind, informally, asking them about Ashley? I'm curious, you know, to see if she was, uh, abrasive as a student too."

"I'll see," she said. "I've got a lot to take care of today, and these interruptions aren't helping. What exactly was it that you wanted?"

"Gordon Greenleaf told me about the judge's research, but he said you could give me more information—particularly with regard to Melvin Haver's death."

"I see." She seemed to consider this for a moment, then asked, "How much do you know about Apostle Bay's founding?"

"Just the general stuff. A company from Boston financed a group to come here in the early 1800s or so—"

"1836."

"Okay. So the group was here to capitalize on the early mining and timber. They arrived by canoe, twelve men led by Randolph Sorenson. That's why we got the name Apostle Bay. Wasn't one of them a priest or something who named the town because there were twelve?"

"Father Benoit. He spoke Ojibwa and was their interpreter."

"Right. So these guys arrived and established the town as a shipping hub for iron and other metals coming out of the ground west of here. The town grew up around the port. That sound about right?"

"There's a lot more to it than that, Vince."

"Yeah, I know. But I have to pick up my daughter pretty soon, so maybe we could just skip the . . ." I saw the peeved look returning. ". . . uh, I mean, maybe you could summarize and then explain about this document the judge was searching for."

She glared at me the way I expect she did at her most inept students.

"Judge Sorenson started off doing family research and genealogy," she said. "His interest was spurred when he discovered Randolph Sorenson's journals in his parents' belongings after they died. They're a fascinating record of his ancestor's vision of capitalizing on the region's mineral boom. The diaries detail how he assembled an exploratory team and came to Northern Michigan in the mid-nineteenth century.

"The journals list supplies they purchased, laborers they hired, how much they paid for the land, etcetera. Sorenson's personality—shrewd, egotistical, and driven—comes out in the writing. He gambled hugely to gain advantage over rival explorers. He eventually won a monopoly on shipping. The success brought him wealth, and at one time he was the second largest landholder in this region.

"As you and most people know, there were twelve men in that first journey: a trapper from the Soo who was their guide, and he had an ax to grind against Sorenson's main competition; there was also Sorenson; a surveyor-geologist; two boatmen; Father Benoit: and six young laborers, the youngest of whom was Melvin Haver."

"Monty's ancestor?" I asked.

"Right."

I surreptitiously glanced at my watch. "Okay, so these guys came in, did their thing, and Apostle Bay became a city."

She sighed. "That's the general idea."

"And the judge has some journals that describe how everything happened."

"With incredible detail," she said.

"So . . . the document that was going to stop the development?"

"The judge didn't know if there *was* a document. I think he was grasping for something because he was angry with city's plans. He kept saying he wanted to fix things."

"What, exactly, did he think existed?"

"*Hoped,* Vince. *Hoped* existed. You need to know a bit more of the history. Melvin Haver was a fourteen-year-old kid at the time he was hired—the youngest of the twelve.

According to the journals, Melvin became Sorenson's right-hand man. Sorenson gave him more and more responsibility and seemed to think of him kind of like a son. There is a reference in one of the journals that implies—now remember, this was the judge's interpretation, and it's vague—it implied that around 1853, when Melvin Haver was thirty, Sorenson gave him a parcel of land as a wedding gift. The journal doesn't describe the land, but we know that Haver built a house around that time that was located where Explorer's Park is now. So—"

"So the judge figured his ancestor gave that land to Melvin Haver."

"Right," she said, but she held up a hand to check my excitement. "However, Melvin Haver and Randolph Sorenson later had a falling-out, and after that point the journals always refer to the land as owned by the Sorenson family. We could find no other references to the wedding gift, or change of land ownership, and no titles or deeds showing the gift. Vince, it's just not likely. I tend to think that Sorenson had been thinking about giving the land as a wedding gift, or something like that, and it never happened."

My conversation with Leisure Suit yesterday came back to mind.

"Did the falling-out have anything to do with Melvin Haver stealing money from Sorenson?"

Her eyes registered surprise. "You *do* know a little bit of local history. Yes, but it wasn't Sorenson he stole the money from. According to the journals and early news reports, Melvin Haver skimmed profits from Boston Properties— that's the financiers who supported the venture. Sorenson discovered this and confronted Haver. Rather than go to jail, Melvin Haver killed himself."

"And he did it near the Manitou River," I said. "Where the judge was found hanging yesterday."

"In the same general vicinity, yes. That's also where Haver's house was."

I took a moment to absorb this, surprised at the accuracy of Phil Ross.

"Well, that explains why there's bad blood between Haver and the judge, even four generations later."

"Yes, it does. And, Vince, I think the judge's research was only going to make things worse."

"Worse?"

"The money Haver stole was never recovered. Randolph Sorenson paid back the company, so Melvin's wife and family wouldn't be held responsible. If that really happened, maybe Melvin's wife gave back the land, as an exchange for Sorenson's paying off the debt. We do know that she moved into town with her two children after Melvin's suicide."

"That might explain why Monty Haver blew up at the judge. The last thing he probably wanted was someone dredging this up again."

"I agree," she said.

"Where are the journals now?"

"I don't know," Patrice said. "I tried to convince the judge to leave them here in the vault, but he wouldn't."

"And you couldn't find them at his house?"

"No," she said. "We couldn't find them. Or his notes."

"Who else knew about them?" I asked.

"Gordon Greenleaf asked me the same thing. Myself, of course. And his personal secretary."

"Elaine Novak?"

"I don't know her name. She only came here with him once."

"Anyone else?"

"He wasn't keeping it a secret. Far from it."

"Do you know about the vandalism at the cemetery?"

She nodded.

"What do you think about that?"

"I think I wouldn't want to be Monty Haver right now," she said.

I was out the door and ten minutes late for Glory when I realized I'd forgotten to ask Patrice about Phil Ross' story and the previous cemetery vandalism.

Chapter Twenty-one

Mom stood waiting on the porch, a bundled up Glory in her arms, when I arrived.

Chrysanthemums lined the walk from her porch to the driveway, plants she slaved over during the summer, pinching them back until they spread into bushy clusters of purple and gold pom-poms that always signaled the end of summer vacation.

Mom came off the porch and pulled the rear door open on my Bronco before I'd shifted to park. She fitted Glory into her car seat.

"Sorry I'm late, but—"

"Don't worry about it," she said. She snapped Glory into the safety belt, gave her a quick caress on the cheek, and said, "See you later." Then she tossed Glory's bag in and slammed the door.

"Hi, Glory."

"Hi, Papa," she said with a yawn.

My daughter, her dark hair peeking out from her hood,

had that dreamy look that usually appeared moments before she dropped off. She'd be asleep before we reached home, I thought, and I wondered if Mom had seen it too. Probably that was why she'd rushed us off.

I'd driven about two blocks when Glory roused and told me she'd forgotten Big Dog, her favorite stuffed animal. In the rearview mirror I saw a growing anxiety in her eyes and knew she was heading toward a possible meltdown. I pulled over to the curb and searched through her bag.

Glory was insistent. "Big Dog is at Nana's."

This was one of those moments when I knew I should tell her we'd get Big Dog tomorrow—maybe explain that Grandma needed Big Dog's company this afternoon, find some way to reason with her—but I just didn't want to deal with it.

"Back to Grandma's," I said, relieved to see Glory settle down.

When I turned onto Mom's block, I saw the chief's black Crown Victoria in her driveway. The chief was climbing the porch stairs to her door.

I pulled in behind his vehicle, left the Bronco idling, and jogged to the house.

"Vince, what are you doing here?"

I noticed he'd removed his tie and that in one hand he held mom's platter, sans cookies. He was halfway trying to hide it from me, but at the same time you could see he realized that was foolish.

"Glory left something behind," I answered. "What are you doing here?"

"I was just in the neighborhood and thought I'd check on your mom and return this."

"Chief, it's been a year now since Eagle's Cliff. I think she's over it."

"Of course she is," he said.

Mom's front door opened. She'd changed from the jeans and flannel shirt she'd been wearing minutes ago to a pair of slacks and a sweater, and she looked surprised to see me.

"I thought I heard voices out here."

"Glory left Big Dog," I said.

"Oh, let me check."

She disappeared into the house, and the chief turned to me.

"Why do you keep baiting Detective Freeman?" he asked. "Every time you do that, you put me in a bad position."

"Maybe because he deserves it?" I said.

Mom came back out the door.

"Here it is," she said. She handed me the black and white dog, a replica of a Siberian husky that had once been soft and fluffy but was now stiff with dried drool. "I don't know how we could have forgotten this."

"Thanks," I said.

She looked at the chief, then at me. "Is everything okay?" she asked.

"No, his detective—"

"Everything's fine," the chief interrupted. "Good-bye, Vince."

"Yeah, um, okay," I said. "Thanks for Big Dog."

I retreated to my car and heard the cell phone chirping as I opened the door.

Chapter Twenty-two

Feeling like a bonehead, I pulled away rather than answer the phone in Mom's driveway. I drove the three blocks my father had walked almost every day of his career to St. Luke's Hospital, parked in the rear corner of the lot, and then checked Glory.

A lock of dark hair had escaped from her hood, curling past her closed eyes and across her cheek, reaching almost to her cute, slightly parted lips. Big Dog rose and fell rhythmically on her chest. Her legs, bent over the car seat, were crossed at the ankles. I pulled a fleece blanket from her backpack and covered her, tucking it loosely around her sides. I considered closing my eyes and taking a brief rest myself but knew that if I did, I'd lose the afternoon.

I opened my cell and saw the call had been from Ashley. I tried her back and left a message when she didn't pick up.

Next I called Rhonda Wentworth to see if Elaine Novak had shown up at the courthouse yet. Elaine probably knew better than anyone else what was going on with the judge before he died.

"Hi, Vince," Rhonda said. "You won't find Monty. He took the rest of the day off soon after you left this morning. I don't think he's doing so well."

"I don't blame him," I said. "But that's not why I called. Has Elaine shown up?"

"No. I tried her at home—twice. There's no answer there. I'm getting worried. Yesterday I figured she was just upset over the judge's death, but it's not like her to miss work. And, Vince?" She lowered her voice. "I called the sheriff's office, and they looked up her ex-husband, Reggie. He was released from the county jail a month ago."

"Where does she live? I'll swing by her house."

"It's just up the street from the courthouse," Rhonda said. "In one of those old homes converted into apartments." She gave me the address.

"I'll go check it out. And, Rhonda, I think you ought to call Detective Greenleaf and tell him about Reggie Novak."

Five minutes later I parked across from the address Rhonda gave me. The house was an imposing, weather-beaten Victorian rising on a mound of earth six or eight feet higher than the road. A crumbling slate-and-mortar retaining wall held back the yard. I craned my neck to see the building's peaked roof and second-story windows and decided the place had probably been elegant in its day but was in dire need of repair now. Paint peeled from the window trim and soffits, a shutter was missing, and the porch sagged. There was no garage, nor driveway, probably because the house was built before there were cars. I got the feeling that the entire structure and yard were poised to slide into the street.

I dialed Elaine's number. There was no answer.

I swung around and checked on Glory. She snored lightly. I could dash across the street, check the apartment to see if there was any sign of Elaine, and be back before Glory stirred. I'd leave the engine running to keep the heat on.

I looked at the house again, double-checked Glory in the mirror, and bolted before I had a chance to second-guess what a stupid move that was.

I crossed the road and ran up a narrow concrete stair cut into the retaining wall. The stairs treads tilted, pushed up in spots by years of frost heave. There was a broken sidewalk at the top, partly hidden under orange and brown leaves. I glanced once more at the idling Bronco, then followed the concrete path around behind the house.

In the back, three wooden steps led up to an apartment entrance. Two flowerpots, home to dried stalks, bracketed the stair. A mailbox hung on the house next to the door. I checked; it was empty.

I couldn't find a doorbell, so I opened the storm door to knock. The inner door was cracked open. Curtains blocked the door's window, and I couldn't see inside.

I looked over one shoulder, I'm not sure why, maybe thinking Elaine might have stepped outside for a moment and I'd see her in the yard. But besides a dilapidated storage shed and a clothesline strung between two T-shaped poles, the yard was empty.

I rapped on the door. It creaked open.

"Hello," I called. "Elaine?"

The door opened into a disaster zone. Bowls, plates, and pots covered the vinyl floor, as if the two empty cupboards on the wall had spit them out. The table lay overturned. Catalogs and other junk mail were strewn about in the mess. White powder, probably flour, coated everything. I pushed the door a bit farther, looking into the kitchen.

"Hello," I called again. "Anyone home?"

I pulled out my cell to call 911 and heard a sound, or thought I did. It might have come from one of the other apartments.

"Elaine? Are you okay?"

I started backing out the door and then stopped, thinking about what had happened last year when Gordon rushed into a burning house to save a kid and I'd been unable to follow. What if Elaine was in the other room and needed immediate help? And what would I tell the operator?

"Hello!" I yelled.

Silence.

"Is anyone here?"

This is stupid, I decided. I took a deep breath, picked my way across the kitchen mess as fast as possible, passed into the hall beyond, turned left, and caught a brief glimpse of something moving. Then the lights went out.

Chapter Twenty-three

Was I in my kayak again? I felt as if I was hanging up-side down, and I couldn't breathe.

Then the world seemed to flip. I caught a glimpse of gray light. My nose felt as if it had been shoved into my face, my forehead throbbed, and my teeth ached. I still couldn't breathe, and I started to panic.

When I tried to move my hands, to press against the pain, they didn't get the message. Everything was distorted, slug-gish, as if I was drowning in syrup. I needed oxygen.

"Vince!"

The voice was far away, muted. I heard it again.

"Vince! What . . . ?"

The pain sharpened. I wanted to fall back into the murky, surreal place where it didn't hurt so badly.

"Hey, man, you okay?"

A hand gripped my shoulder.

"Can you hear me?"

Everything was starting to come back: my name, where I

was. The room grew lighter. Someone pulled me up until I was sitting. It was twin Gordons who merged into one as my eyes focused.

"Hey, buddy, what happened?"

"I'm . . . man, I've got a wicked headache." The words sounded funny in my head, distant and muffled.

"You're a mess," he said. "Definitely a broken nose."

I blinked a few more times. Just moving my eyes hurt. I couldn't breathe through my nose and still felt a bit as if I was underwater. I touched my face, and my hand came away wet and sticky.

"What happened?"

"You tell me," he said.

"I don't—what are you doing here?"

"We got a call from the courthouse to check out this place. Something about a missing woman."

Elaine Novak. The name pushed its way through the fog in my head.

"When I pulled up, I could have sworn I saw you driving away," Gord said. "Did Deb drop you off? Is she nearby? Can I call her?"

I thought a moment, trying to recall how I'd gotten here.

"No—"

"You sure? You don't look like you're all the way with us yet."

"Yeah."

He picked his way back into the kitchen and returned with a dishrag. "Here."

I dabbed gingerly at my face. The blood was running back into my throat now. I hawked and spat into the rag.

"Odd," Gord said. "I was sure it was your Bronco heading up the street when I arrived. There was a car between us, but there aren't too many Broncos around town with a bright yellow kayak on top. Anyway, what the heck happened here?"

Driving, I thought. I blinked again, trying to get my brain to work. Greenleaf squatted next to me now, studying my face with a grimace that made me feel worse.

"Glory," I tried to say, but my mouth wouldn't seem to work. "Huh?"

"Glory," I said, rolling over onto my knees. I grabbed his arm for support.

"Whoa, slow down, buddy."

I pulled myself up, hanging on to him and the wall. The house seemed to sway.

"Glory," I said. "I left her . . . in my car."

Greenleaf studied me a moment longer, and then I saw the information click into place. He let go of me and blasted out the door. I stumbled after him, my arms, legs, and mind still moving in slow motion.

When I got to the concrete stairs out front, Greenleaf was already at his car, talking into his radio. My Bronco was nowhere in sight.

"Which way did they go?" I called.

He pointed—up the street, to my left. I spat another mouthful of blood, stumbled down the stairs, and turned up the street in that direction. I felt stupid, helpless, and ready to tear the head off whoever had taken my daughter.

"Wait, Vince!" I heard him call.

I kept running. At the first intersection I stopped in the middle and looked in all directions, spinning, for some reason believing I'd see taillights and my kayak like a bright yellow flag. I was standing there, still turning from street to street, when Greenleaf pulled up.

"Get in," he said. "We've got everybody looking, Vince. They won't get far. Your car's too recognizable."

"Unless they get to the highway."

"They do that; the state police have them. We'll find her."

I looked around, feeling helpless, feeling as if I should be running, checking all the side streets.

"Get in," he said again.

I looked down each street again, then jogged over to Greenleaf's car. My cell rang as I reached for the door handle. It took a moment to register what the sound was. I settled into Gord's sedan, and then I pulled it out of my pocket. The screen showed the call was from Ashley. Not now, I thought, and I silenced the ringer.

Greenleaf handed me another rag. "For your nose," he said.

I wiped the blood while he started cruising up and down the neighborhood streets.

My cell rang again. Ashley again. I silenced it.

Three blocks west of Elaine Novak's apartment Greenleaf spotted my SUV parked down a side street. He gunned through the right turn and screeched to a stop in front of the Bronco, almost giving me a second face-plant as he did.

I flew out of his cruiser, moving on automatic, yanking open the Bronco's back door to see Glory.

My daughter was still snoozing in her car seat as if nothing had changed. I climbed into the seat next to her, popped her safety belt, and gently lifted her free, pulling her to me as she stirred awake. I kissed her head, and when I had her against my chest, such relief washed over me that nothing else in the world existed at that moment but my daughter, my lovely, lovely little girl. I settled into the vehicle's backseat and cradled her.

Chapter Twenty-four

"Vince, you okay?"

Ashley stood in the road about five feet away and stared at me as if I was some kind of freak. I turned away from her and caught sight of my face in the rearview mirror.

I looked horrific—blood smeared from my nose down to my chin, both eyes purple and nearly swollen shut, my hair sticking up wildly. My teeth felt numb, tingly. I ran my tongue across them, glad to feel none missing.

Glory pushed herself away and opened her mouth in a wide yawn. She blinked and did a toddler's version of a double take, looking at my face. I'd smeared blood on her coat and in her hair. For some strange reason—the absurdity of the situation, her goofy look of surprise, my relief, who knows?—I half cried and half laughed and snorted out more blood.

"I saw your car here," Ashley said. "I heard on the scanner about Glory's kidnapping. Then I saw she was okay here. I tried calling you."

I wiped my face again with Gordon's rag and looked around outside. Reds and blues flashed from two city patrol cars parked near us. I heard a siren nearing, a burst of radio static, and voices from the patrol cars. Gordon directed two cops in front of us; then they took off toward the nearest houses.

Relief at Glory's safety was starting to give way to anger.

"Did you see who was driving?" I asked Ashley.

"No," she said. "Your car was parked here, the engine running, when I came by. I looked in and saw that your daughter was asleep, so I thought it best not to wake her, just wait for the police."

"You called the cops?" I asked.

"Well, after I couldn't get you, I called 9-1-1. You guys pulled up a minute later. Is there . . . I mean, can I do anything for you?"

"Yeah, help me find who took my daughter."

"Excuse me, miss."

An EMT took Ashley by one elbow and guided her away. Then he looked me up and down. "Look's like you went a few rounds in the ring with somebody a lot bigger."

"Feels like it too," I said.

"It'll be way worse tonight after the shock wears off. Let's get you over to the wagon and clean you up."

He reached for Glory, but I pulled her against me and slid out of the backseat.

Now fully awake, she pointed behind us and said, "Amby-lance. Papa need amby-lance."

"Yep." I said. "Papa needs the ambulance. Somebody else is going to need it too."

Matthew Williams

My legs almost gave out when I stood, but the EMT had been ready, and he grabbed my arm.

As he helped me over, I thought I caught a flash of light and winced, sure that it meant Ashley was back on the job, taking photos.

Chapter Twenty-five

Glory used the plastic stethoscope the emergency room doc gave her to listen for a heartbeat in the walls and in the cabinets of our examining room at St. Luke's.

She'd been full of importance since the ride in the ambulance, which I had at first refused, until watching tears well up in her eyes. At the moment I'd do just about anything for her, including swallowing my pride. The EMTs had been awesome, showing her the equipment, giving her a pair of latex gloves and goggles, and letting her stick a few Band-Aids on me.

Right now I sat on an examination table, watching her with alternate eyes as I moved an ice bag from side to side. She was babbling to herself as she explored. I'm not sure how the whole situation was affecting her. Obviously she'd basked in the attention, but there also seemed to be an underlying knowledge that this wasn't normal.

The emergency room doc, a mid-sixties bear of a man with a wild beard who was known around town as the nut who always drove his Harley to work, even in blizzards, had been a colleague of my father's. He was old-school enough to basically tell me I should take two aspirin and quit my whining. He confirmed what everyone else had been so willing to tell me: that my schnoz was broken, I had two wicked-looking black eyes that were going to be ugly for a while, and that I probably had a minor concussion. In his opinion, nothing a bag of frozen vegetables and intestinal fortitude wouldn't solve. Unless I was barfing, he said, he wasn't going to waste the energy of an MRI on me.

I still couldn't remember what had happened. He told me that was normal for a guy who walked into walls.

What he lacked in sympathy for me, he more than made up for in attention to Glory. She called him Dr. Ben, and he'd pulled a toy doctor kit from a wall cabinet and handed it to her. The kits were an annual donation from Judge Sorenson to the hospital, given to all children who came into the emergency room. They included a red box with stethoscope, reflex hammer, thermometer, plastic scissors, and that tape that sticks only to itself. Dr. Ben told her to keep an eye on me, and if I complained too much, she should use the hammer to test my reflexes.

Glory was testing it out now, lightly whacking the walls and then listening for a response.

One came, from over by the door. We both turned to see Gordon, a fist raised, ready to knock on the doorjamb again. Glory tapped. He tapped back, and she giggled.

"Morse code," I said.

"How are you doing?"

"Other than feeling like I was clobbered with a baseball bat? I'll survive."

"How about . . . ?" He nodded Glory's way.

"She's resilient."

"Good," he said. "By the way, it wasn't a baseball bat. It was a wooden door, and not one of those hollow composite ones either, but a heavy, solid bugger, if that makes you feel any better."

"Makes me feel great."

I tried to picture Elaine's apartment again, but other than the hazy glimpse I'd had while stumbling out, I couldn't recall much about the place.

"It looks like you walked in on someone. They must have been hiding in the next room, and when you passed through the kitchen, they slammed the door into you, probably knocking you out cold for a few minutes. Then they took off. That's my guess."

"Anybody see anything?"

"No," he said. "The other apartments in the house were empty. We canvassed the neighborhoods behind Elaine Novak's house and all the way over to where we found your Bronco, but most people weren't home. No witnesses."

"Bummer."

"The state police have your vehicle at the barracks. Chances are good that whoever took your car left something behind—prints, fibers, something. They'll find it."

"Thanks. Wonder why they'd take it a few blocks and then ditch it."

"Probably because of your scanner. I'll bet they heard the call go out and realized there was no way they could get out of town without being spotted. Probably jumped out as soon as they heard it."

Glory went over to Gord. "Checkup time," she said.

Gordon squatted down and let her hold the stethoscope against his forehead.

"Did you see who was driving your papa's car?" he asked her.

"Mama does sometimes," she said.

"She slept through the whole thing," I added.

"Whoever stole your car probably didn't realize Glory was there until they heard it on the scanner, and then I'd guess they freaked. Good thing she slept through it, though. Her being awake and seeing the person might have complicated things. . . ."

Gord let that hang, his little way of telling me that Glory and I got lucky. I felt like punching something, maybe myself, but wasn't up for more pain.

Glory put a Band-Aid on Gordon and checked his temperature. "No fever," she said with authority.

"Thanks," Gordon said. He pulled her into a quick hug, and that brief show of emotion from him magnified my guilt.

Glory squirmed free after a moment.

"Your daddy is silly, Glory," he said.

"I know," she said. "Silly, silly."

Glory moved away and resumed tapping the walls.

"Did you . . . ? Elaine wasn't . . . um . . . in there, was she?"

"No," he said.

"Was there any sign she was . . . you know . . . ?"

"Not at first glance," he said.

"Did Rhonda Wentworth tell you about the ex-husband?"

"Yeah," he said. "The chief's interviewing him as we speak."

"You found him that quickly?"

"Wasn't too hard," Gordon said. "The probation office gave us his address. He's a possibility, but I had another thought. What do you know about—?"

Gord stopped when we heard voices behind him. My mom appeared, along with Dr. Ben.

"See, Loretta?" the doctor said. "They're both okay."

"Thanks, Ben," she said. "See you at Explorer's Park tonight, then?"

"Wouldn't miss it," he said.

Mom put a hand on Gordon's shoulder in greeting as she passed, then pushed into the room and grabbed me in a bear hug.

"Ow," I said. "That hurts!"

She backed away enough to scan my face without letting go of my shoulders. "Good," she said.

"A face only a mother could love, right?"

She smiled, then bent to Glory and scooped her up.

"Time for checkup, Nana," Glory said, showing off her stethoscope.

"Sure thing, Dr. Glory," Mom said.

Gordon pushed himself away from the wall. "Give me a call tonight, Vince. When you get home."

"When can I have my car back?"

"Maybe a week."

"Can't they move it along a bit faster?"

"Call me," he said, and from his tone I knew he had something he wanted to discuss with me alone.

Gordon left. My mom had lifted Glory onto the examination table beside me, and the tissue paper crinkled as Glory climbed to a kneeling position so she'd be at eye level with her Nana.

I put my arm around the little buckaroo, feeling the need to touch her again. She tried to fend me off, annoyed that I was interrupting Grandma's checkup. I didn't give in, squeezing her to me as she checked her toy thermometer.

Chapter Twenty-six

"What *were* you thinking?" Deb asked.

We were in our kitchen. Deb, leaning back against the counter, had her arms folded across her chest. The accusatory look on her face said much more than those four words.

She was still dressed her in her school clothes—black slacks, ivory blouse, and autumn-colored vest—and looked exhausted. Being mom, teacher, volunteer, and protest leader was taking its toll.

Glory, my mother, and I had been drinking tea and playing doctor again when Deb arrived home from school. Mom left soon after, but not before pulling Deb aside and whispering something—I can only guess it was on the order of explaining my stupidity.

I sat at the table now, moving a bag of frozen corn from eye to eye. If anything, my face was more swollen. The skin felt taut.

On Deb's right, near the sliding glass door that overlooked the beach, a stack of protest signs leaned against the wall. Songs from a *Dora the Explorer* video drifted in from our living room, where Deb had parked Glory after smothering her in hugs and kisses and submitting to a checkup that involved more of Deb's examining Glory than the other way around.

"Obviously I wasn't thinking," I said, trying to look at her through one swollen eyelid.

Deb lowered her voice. "What if you hadn't found the car?"

"I've already asked myself that same question a hundred times. I know I was an idiot. I've run through all the disastrous what-if scenarios. I'm going to keep kicking myself for quite some time, okay? So I don't need you to do it right now too."

I shifted the corn to cover both my eyes so I wouldn't have to look at her.

"I think we should look into day care again," she said.

"No."

Deb came across the room and sat next to me. "Face it, Vince. You can't give up work. And you shouldn't have to. But you can't keep dragging Glory around while you're doing it. That's not what we talked about when you went part-time."

"I don't drag her around all the time."

"Yes, you do."

"No, I don't," I said. I sat up, moving too fast and getting a head rush. I stifled a moan and sat back.

"In the last two days she's found a dead body and been kidnapped. What's next?"

"C'mon, Deb. That's not fair, and you know it. I wasn't working when we found the judge."

"And today?" she said.

"I think we've already established that today I was an idiot."

"You'll get no argument from me on that."

"Thanks," I said, and I reapplied the frozen vegetables. "Now how about a little love for me? I'm hurting here."

"It's pretty hard to love a face that looks like that," she said, but her voice was softer and had a twinge of pity in it. She took my hand and squeezed it.

A knock at the back door interrupted what I'd hoped was going to be some sympathy time.

"It's Tony," Deb said, looking at her watch and then standing to answer the door. "He came to get some of the signs."

Deb pulled the slider open and let in her friend and colleague Tony Wittmer.

"Ouch," Wittmer said when he saw me. "Who'd you run into?"

Glory came running at the sound of his voice. "Tony!" she yelled. "Look at this."

She showed him her stethoscope and hammer. Although Tony's known Deb for some time, since they both taught at a school in Grand Rapids, and he's become my friend—in a loose sense of the word—over the last year, I still get jealous at the rise he gets from Glory. He has a way with her that I haven't matched. Deb calls it the funny-uncle syndrome. He can be all silly, never having to discipline or draw a line or be the bad guy. That's my job.

I dropped the veggies, tried sitting up a little straighter, and put on my tough-guy act.

"Hey, little girl," he said. "That's cool stuff."

"Want to see something cooler, Tony?" she said. "Look at Papa's nose."

I tried to crack a little smile without moving any other part of my face.

"I see," he said. "Very cool. Did you do that?"

"Tony!" she squealed. He picked her up and spun her around, then put her down.

"So what did happen, Vince? An interview go bad?"

"I walked into a door," I said. "It's nothing."

"Yeah, right. Anyway, I'm here to grab some of those signs."

"Deb, I thought this vigil wasn't a political event," I said. "Are you sure bringing the signs is a good thing?"

"The rumor is that Jack Reynolds will make an appearance and a speech at the eulogy. I guess he's somehow convinced the judge's nephew that he's the best one to speak on the family's behalf. We just want to be prepared to apply a little pressure if we need to."

"But don't you think . . . ?"

"Don't worry, Vince," Wittmer said. "Deb has a plan. I don't think we'll need the signs beyond having them for show."

"A plan, huh? This I can't wait to see."

Chapter Twenty-seven

We helped Tony load four signs. Deb tried to insist I stay at the table, showing that she obviously doesn't understand male egos. The activity made me light-headed, and I dropped back into a kitchen chair once Tony departed.

"You can't wait to see my plan, huh?" Deb said. "Does that mean you're planning to come?"

"Sure. I'll have Dr. Glory with me in case I need any care."

I didn't add that I also hoped to connect with Ashley and share what little info I'd learned about the judge's death.

"But—"

"Really, I'm fine. I'll keep some frozen broccoli in the car."

"Didn't you listen to anything I said earlier? Glory shouldn't be there."

"Sure, she should. It will be a good experience for her. It'll be kind of like a parade, what with the candles and all. I think she'll like it."

"A parade? Are you nuts?"

"Deb, it will be fine. She should see her mom in action

and the good things you do. Besides, she'll be with me. If there's any problem, we'll just leave. Okay?"

Deb hesitated. "Vince, I don't think—"

"It'll be fine," I said.

Deb looked at me and then laughed.

"What?"

"You know you're going to spend the entire time explaining what happened to your face."

"I'll wear a hat and sunglasses. Nobody will know."

"Right," she said. She kissed the top of my head and then went to the refrigerator. "I've got some time; let's see what we can pull off for dinner."

While Deb cooked, I gave her a more detailed version of our afternoon. She made the same jump I did: Jack Reynolds now had a motive. I drained her excitement with the news that he also had an alibi.

Glory came into the room while we talked. "Ready for checkup?" she asked me.

"Sure," I said. "See if you can figure out why I'm so ugly."

Glory tapped my thighs with her reflex hammer, and I jerked my legs around.

Deb came over, set a plate in front of Glory's booster seat, and lifted our daughter into place. She asked, "Did anyone think to check the women's shelter for Elaine?"

"No," I said. After a moment I added, "But they wouldn't tell us if she was there anyway."

"You could leave a message for her," Deb said. "They'd get it to her if she is there."

I nodded, liking the idea.

"I'll check with Sarah at the vigil tonight too," Deb said. "She's on the shelter's board. She might even know Elaine."

Glory held her sippy cup toward me. "Want medicine?"

"Thanks, honey," I said, taking it from her and pretending to drink.

"Drink up," she said, a stern look crossing her face.

My little Nurse Ratched, I thought. I held up the cup and made gulping sounds, then returned it.

"Speaking of Sarah," I said, "we need to work on her about running for judge. Guess who announced his candidacy today?"

Deb said, "I hope it was somebody with sense."

"Rudy Clark."

"The prosecutor?"

"Yeah. In fact, I have to whip together a short piece on it tonight and e-mail it to Lou."

"That's not so bad, is it?"

"If he wins, they'll have to widen the courthouse doors to make room for his big head. Trust me, Sarah needs to get involved."

"It's in the works," Deb said. "I called Lucy DeMott to see if she'd cover the vigil for the TV news, and I spiced it up by mentioning the rumor that's Sarah's considering a run for judge."

"I suppose Sarah doesn't know that."

"Not yet," Deb said. "But she will tonight."

Chapter Twenty-eight

At Explorer's Park I hung a few steps inside the tree line near the picnic area, hoping to stay as inconspicuous as possible. Besides wearing a ball cap and glasses, I pulled up the collar on my fleece jacket, as much to stay warm as to hide.

A nippy breeze came in off Superior, and if it didn't die back soon, I thought the candlelight vigil was going to be without light.

Behind me in the trees a solitary flycatcher signaled occasionally, it's plaintive *pee-oh-wee* call making for easy identification. It would head south soon, I knew, searching for warmer places and trees that weren't shedding their leaves.

Glory had gone, hand in hand with Deb, to the pavilion in the center of the grassy picnic area. That's where SCALD was gathering to organize the event. There were about fifty people already and a steady stream of cars pulling into the parking lot. Most were empty-handed and bundled up against the dropping temperature. A handful carried signs protesting the development, but they seemed subdued, even a little embarrassed. Several families brought children too. I looked for Sarah Dodge but didn't see her in the crowd. Maybe she'd caught wind of Deb's plan.

Tony Wittmer was moving through the group, handing out candles. I was surprised to see Rhonda Wentworth helping him, as I didn't think she came to outdoor events. Ashley looked to be interviewing someone near a corner of the pavilion.

The sun was edging below the western treetops, and its magenta hues matched those of the sugar maple leaves. The sky was clear, and that meant we'd probably have another frost tonight.

I scanned the area, looking for someone who might be the judge's nephew, and noticed that the cops were out in force. Archie Freeman rode his mountain bike through the lot and disappeared down the path that led toward the Apostle Memorial. Two patrol officers stood by the park's entrance, chatting to each other. I caught sight of Mom and the chief standing back in the tree line like myself, about forty yards away.

Lucy DeMott pulled in, driving the TV station's car, and a lot of heads swung her way. Everyone wants to get on television, I thought.

Deb had told me that the group's plan was to light their candles after sunset and proceed silently down the woodchip path, cross the arched bridge that I'd chased Glory over the day before, and go into the memorial grove where the judge had died. A local minister was going to give a brief eulogy there, and others could add their own comments. A group from the high school chorale planned to sing "Amazing Grace."

I was supposed to stay near and snag Glory when the procession started.

"Just as I thought," a deep voice said behind me. "Trying to hide your face tonight?"

I jumped at the sound, then turned to find Gordon. "Where did you come from?" I asked.

"Down by the lake," he said. "I followed the river path back up to here. Steelhead should be running soon."

"How about a little warning next time?"

He smiled, and I could tell he'd enjoyed startling me.

"You surprised by the turnout?" I asked.

The parking lot was now full, and cars were parking on the grass near the park entrance.

"No," he said. "We expected it."

"Why so many cops? Worried the protesters will get out of hand?"

"Should I be?"

"No."

"Good."

"What was it you wanted to tell me at the hospital?"

Gordon smiled and greeted a lady passing near us with three children in tow. They were coming out of the playground and heading over to the pavilion, one of the kids complaining that he was hungry. In the distance, ore pellets slid down a metal chute into a ship's hold, the whooshing sound carrying across the bay.

"How well do you know Ashley Adams?" he asked.

"Not that well. She's been at the *Chronicle* a few weeks."

"What do you think of her?"

"She's headstrong, cuts corners, and is willing to stab you in the back, but she seems smart too. She'll outgrow the other stuff once she realizes we're not against each other. Why do you ask?"

He wasn't looking at me; instead, his eyes roamed over

the crowd. But I got the feeling he was debating whether or not to tell me something.

"Gord?"

"Interesting coincidence that she showed up at your car this afternoon," he said.

"Not really. I'd promised to call her much earlier with information she needed for a story, but I got sidetracked. She was probably ticked off and pulled over when she saw my Bronco to give me a piece of her mind. She's like that."

"Maybe."

"Who cares why she was there? I'm bummed she didn't see who'd stolen my car."

"Uh-huh."

"What? You think she saw something and is keeping it to herself?"

I could see her doing just that if she'd thought it would enhance a story. But she'd seemed genuinely upset when I arrived, not as if she was playing me.

"I asked her for a hair sample this afternoon, just to eliminate any evidence the forensic lab finds in your car. She balked."

"Sure. It seems a little intrusive, don't you think?"

"Yes, except I said it was to eliminate possibilities—the same reason I took samples from you and Deb and Glory. I only asked Ashley because she told us she'd been in the car to check on Glory's safety."

I shrugged, not sure what he was getting at.

"Did she mention to you why she called 9-1-1?" Gord said.

I thought back to that afternoon. "Yeah. She heard about the kidnapping on the scanner."

"Uh-huh."

"Would you get to the point, Gord?"

"She didn't have a police scanner."

"I know," I said. "She doesn't own one. I assumed she heard the scanner in my car while she was checking on Glory."

"You're probably right."

"What else?"

"She didn't have a car there."

"She must have walked," I said.

"Must have," Gord said. "I just have this feeling that she wasn't being honest, that's all. Let's see what turns up on the forensic report."

Gord nodded toward the parking lot where a sunshine yellow Hummer H2 rolled through the entrance.

"We can talk about it later," he said. "It's time for me to go to work."

Chapter Twenty-nine

Jack Reynolds drove his gas hog through the full parking lot, and I got the feeling he intended to pull up to the pavilion. Instead, he drove onto the grass nearby and parked. A couple SCALD members went for their signs. Gordon slipped past me and walked their way. I saw the chief moving toward the group also.

Mom was still standing on the periphery, and I gave her a quick wave.

All four doors of the H2 swung open. Reynolds came around the vehicle's brush bar and met a taller guy climbing out of the front passenger seat. A city councilman exited from the rear passenger side and joined them. A moment later I was surprised to see Rudy Clark come around the vehicle. I hadn't realized he was a member of Reynolds' posse, though politically it made sense.

The guy who'd been riding shotgun matched Mort Maki's description of Peter Sorenson, not necessarily the dork part, but tall and not much meat on his bones. He slapped his arms, pulled the zipper on his green and white Windbreaker up to his chin, and blew into his hands.

Reynolds said something and laughed before slapping the guy's back.

Lucy DeMott moved out of the crowd toward them. I moved in too, curious to see the judge's heir. I expected Ashley to push her way to the front as well but didn't see her yet.

Most of the people gathered were now watching the spectacle—exactly as Reynolds had planned, I'm sure.

Reynolds was glad-handing everybody in the vicinity when I arrived. The chief, Deb, and Glory came up to the group. Deb whispered something to Glory, and she ran over to me, a candle clutched in each hand. Deb caught my eye and let me know it was time to take our daughter.

I swung Glory up onto my shoulders and listened.

Reynolds told the chief that Peter wanted to lead the procession, since it was his uncle who was being honored. I noticed that he ignored Deb, though she'd organized the event.

Peter didn't look too keen on the idea of leading a parade of mourners. In fact, he looked as if he'd rather climb back into the Hummer and crank up the heat.

"And the signs have to go, Chief," Reynolds said. "Have your men confiscate them."

"Now, Jack, you know I can't—"

"It's called the First Amendment," Deb said, interrupting the chief. "People have a constitutional right to voice their opinions."

Rudy Clark coughed and then stepped forward. "Actually, if you want a legal interpretation—"

Reynolds cut in. "You people don't have the constitutional right to cause more pain for this man." He put a hand on Peter's shoulder and acted as if he could personally feel the man's pain, which at the moment seemed to be based more on stage fright than grief. I noticed his gaze darting among the crowd, as if he'd hoped to find at least one or two people he knew.

Lucy dropped to the ground and scrambled to get her camera rolling. Ashley squeezed her way to the front.

"Actually, Jack," the chief said, "there's not much—"

"We don't want to cause you any more distress," Deb said, approaching Peter directly and putting a hand on his arm. "Some people brought those signs because they're a reflection of your uncle's clearly voiced opinion. But if they make you uncomfortable, we'll leave them here. We understand that it wouldn't be appropriate to politicize tonight's event, especially the eulogy."

She turned to Jack and matched his glare. "Right, Jack?"

I squeezed Glory's foot and whispered, "Your mom's pretty clever."

"Wouldn't think of it," Reynolds said.

"If I could say something," Clark piped in.

At that moment the halogen lamp atop Lucy's camera snapped on. Peter Sorenson, Reynolds, and Clark all threw up their arms to block the blinding light. Glory dropped her candles and must have covered her eyes too. I was happy to be wearing sunglasses.

"Whoops. Sorry about that," Lucy said. She aimed the light down toward their feet.

"Great. It's settled, then," said Deb. "I'll go get you gentlemen some candles, and we'll start the procession. Are you familiar with the park, Mr. Sorenson?"

Peter, obviously blinking spots out of his eyes, turned toward Reynolds for an answer.

"Not to worry," Deb said. "I'll escort you along the path."

She glanced over and winked at me. If my eyes weren't so swollen, I'd have lifted my shades and winked back.

As Deb walked away, Lucy rested her camera on one hip and stepped forward.

"Lucy DeMott, TV news," she said to Peter. She shot out her hand. He seemed reluctant to take it, but she kept it hanging there until he gave her a halfhearted squeeze. "I'm sorry about your uncle. It must be especially tragic since you were here visiting when it happened."

"Uh, yeah, tragic," Peter said.

"I'm putting together a little feature about your late uncle and his philanthropy," she said.

Lucy stepped forward and handed Peter a microphone that was attached to her camera by a red cable. He took it reluctantly.

"Hold it right here," she said, moving his hand to his belly; then she inched his jacket zipper down until his neck showed. "There. Just relax, and talk naturally."

She took a step back and swung the camera onto her shoulder. This time the light was angled down enough not to blind the group. The red RECORD light came on.

"Can you tell me your thoughts about your uncle, Mr. Sorenson? He was very generous to this community."

"Maybe a little—" Peter started.

Ashley stepped forward and yanked the microphone from Peter Sorenson's hand. "Give the guy a break," she said. "His uncle just died. This *is* a memorial service, you know."

Lucy lowered he camera. "Hey, what do you—?"

Reynolds stepped in. "May I?" he asked, gesturing toward the mic. Ashley seemed caught off guard. Reynolds took the microphone and stepped back.

Lucy glared at Ashley, then lifted the camera again and focused this time on Reynolds.

"Ms. DeMott," he said. "Tonight is about Judge Sorenson and how much he was loved by this community. But I'm sure Peter has enough to deal with this evening, such as his grief. So for the moment I'll speak on his behalf about the wonderful contributions the Sorenson family . . ."

Deb and Tony Wittmer came back soon after, carrying a box of candles, and pulled Peter Sorenson aside as Reynolds blathered on. Wittmer passed the candles around, Deb took Peter by one arm and guided him away, and other SCALD members clogged the path as they moved toward the memorial, blocking Reynolds and Clark.

Ashley moved off too, sticking near Peter Sorenson. I was still amazed that she'd yanked Lucy's mic away. It was a bold move, but I wondered if this time she might have ticked off the wrong person.

Chapter Thirty

By the time the candlelight procession fell to order, the sun had passed behind the trees, and I realized the wind had fallen off too.

I squatted and picked up Glory's candles and, according to our compromise, carried one in each hand while she rode on my shoulders.

Rhonda hustled over and touched her flame to each of my candles. Then she grabbed my arm and leaned close. "I heard all about what happened at Elaine's," she said.

"Already?"

"Let me have a look."

She stepped between my arms and pulled off the sunglasses. Since I was balancing a candle in each hand and trying not to burn her, there wasn't much I could do to prevent it.

"Nasty," she said, and then she slipped the glasses back on, thankfully without poking any tender spots.

"Any word from Elaine?" I asked.

"None," she said. "I'm worried. Reggie's a psycho."

"She'll turn up," I said, hoping Deb was right about the shelter.

"I chatted with Monty this evening," she said. "He's going to call you tomorrow to talk. Please try to help him."

Then she flitted away to help others light their candles.

I hung near the back of the procession and watched the little tongues of flame dance in the woods ahead of us, a serpent of light following the path. It had a hypnotic effect on Glory. She rested her chin on my head and then nodded forward into sleep.

At the bridge I peeled away from the procession, blew out my candles, and lowered Glory. I settled her against my chest, and she sighed. Her rhythmic breathing and the dead weight she becomes when thoroughly limp told me she was down for the count.

I cut back through the park, taking a different path from the mourners, figuring we could go back and snooze in the car until Deb was done. We'd just reached the parking lot when that plan went out the window.

Chapter Thirty-one

First I heard the voices behind us, coming from back on the trail and growing louder. A moment later the chief and Gordon broke out of the woods and jogged into the parking lot. Both headed toward their sedans. The chief's white vehicle was closer to us, and he was also several paces behind the athletic Greenleaf, so I cut over toward him.

"What's going on, Chief?"

"Fire," he grunted. "At the women's shelter."

Gord was already in his car, and I heard the engine start.

It can't be a coincidence, I thought. "It's gotta be arson, Chief."

"Vince, I don't have time for this." He opened his door and slid into the seat.

"Anyone hurt?"

The chief slammed his door shut. Gordon's sedan spit gravel as it moved out, and the chief's sedan cranked to life.

I stepped back, wondering how I could get to the fire with Deb's car and not leave her hanging. I cursed the creep who'd taken my Bronco that afternoon. I didn't even have my scanner to listen to the action.

The chief peeled away, his siren shrieking to life. I walked back to Deb's car. If I took it, she'd catch a ride home with Wittmer or someone else and maybe even think I'd taken Glory home. Of course, she'd flip out when she discovered I went to the fire instead.

It was a stupid idea anyway. No way could I just leave Glory in the car again while I stepped out to take photos and see if Elaine was staying there, or if she had the judge's journals.

On the other hand, Ashley was somewhere in the park, and so was our photographer. If I didn't do something, we wouldn't get it covered.

I dug into my jacket for my cell phone and started dialing the *Chronicle*. Lou lived at the place; maybe he'd pick up.

Before I pushed SEND, my mother came out of the woods. I jogged over to her.

"There's a fire at the women's shelter," I said.

"I know. Dale told me."

"Is your car here?"

"Yes," she said.

"Great. Glory's conked out in her car seat. Let me move her to your car, and you take her home. I'm going to the fire."

"And how are you going to get there?"

"Deb's car."

"Vince, your eyes are nearly swollen shut, and you're probably loaded with painkillers. You can't drive."

"Sure, I can. It's not that far."

"And you'd be in the way. Let me take you and Glory home. Dale will give you all the details you need tomorrow."

"I really don't have time for this, Mom."

I gave her a quick rundown on the missing journals, why

they were important, and why they could be at the shelter. She looked at me as if I was out of my mind.

"C'mon, Mom. This fire isn't a coincidence. I've got to get over there and let the chief know. And find out if Elaine was there with the judge's notes."

"Maybe that's not such a good idea," she said. "Look what happened the last time you went searching for her."

"That's why I need your help."

She stared at me for a moment and seemed to be considering.

"Okay," she said. "Go get Glory and anything you need, and make sure you leave Deb a note. You can ride with me."

"But, Mom—"

"You want my help, Vince? That's my offer."

Chapter Thirty-two

The women's shelter is on the western edge of town, about five miles inland from the lake. Police and emergency vehicles had already cordoned off the block by the time we arrived, their flashers creating a light show on the neighbors' vinyl siding.

Halfway down the block a ladder truck sat in front of the antiquated white Victorian home with blue gingerbread trim and large porch framed by blue pillars. Thanks to a generous donation from the judge, the Apostle Bay Women's Center had purchased and renovated the home, converting it to apartments where battered or homeless women and children could stay until their tormentors were sent away, or until they could get back on their feet.

Lights glowed in all the home's windows, and other than the drama of emergency vehicles and rubberneckers, there was no sign of a fire.

Mom pulled over as close as she could get to the scene.

"Give me a few minutes," I said, grabbing my camera and hopping out before she could argue.

I skirted wide of the patrol car blocking the road and headed across a couple of front yards toward the shelter. The chief was standing out front, talking with the fire captain. A firefighter was entertaining four or five children at the city's rescue vehicle. The kids wore pajamas and had most likely been evacuated from the home. Two women huddled nearby, their heads bowed together in discussion. I stopped, pulled off my sunglasses, stuffed them into my coat pocket, then snapped a few pictures of the scene.

I moved closer and saw Gordon in a front window, talking with a woman who I thought was the shelter's manager. I caught the odor of smoke but still didn't see any sign of fire. Radios squawked from the trucks. Diesel engines rumbled.

Gordon came down the front steps, turned to my left, and followed the home's driveway around back. I noticed a canvas fire hose stretching up the drive in that direction.

Moving behind the fire truck to stay clear of the chief, then jogging across the road, I followed Gord behind the house. The narrow driveway cut between the old home and an impassible tangle of lilac bushes.

I stuck to the shadows near the house and came out onto a small parking lot with two cars, a rickety carriage house, its walls and roof leaning precariously to the right but its door still oddly square, and a portable basketball hoop and stand. A firefighter sprayed water into a small apartment Dumpster near the carriage house, while another leaned on a shovel nearby.

I found Gordon squatting atop a small porch, poking around the home's back door. He wore latex gloves.

"Hey, Gord," I said, stepping near the porch. "Everyone okay?"

"Who—" He squinted into the darkness toward me. "Oh. I should've known. Where's Glory?"

"Safe," I said. "With Mom."

Still squatting, he shook his head. "You're unbelievable."

"What was it? Just a Dumpster fire?"

"That's what someone wants us to think."

"Huh?"

"Nothing. You'll have to talk with the chief. He's around front."

"You didn't answer. Is everyone okay?"

"Yeah. The fire was contained out here."

I took a couple steps closer. "What are you looking at?" I asked.

"Vince, do me a favor and take off before the chief comes around here and hands us both our heads."

"I was looking for Elaine Novak. Deb thought she might be staying here."

He sighed. "Would you trust me to do my job?" he said. "I already checked that this afternoon. She was staying here for a few days, but she moved out today."

"Then where is she?"

"We don't know."

"Do you think—?"

"Don't make this hard on me, Vince. This is a crime scene. You've got to scram."

"A crime?"

He stood and with a look of exasperation said, "Scram!"

I nodded, realizing I'd pushed it far enough.

I walked back toward the road, stopping to snap a few photos of the firefighter dousing the Dumpster on my way. Back at the street, I started to cross, thinking I'd better stay clear of the chief, but as I planted my first foot on the road, he turned in my direction and saw me.

He turned back, said something to the fire captain, and then crossed the road toward me. I met him halfway.

"You need to clear out of here."

"I was just on my way," I said.

"Good."

"So what happened?" I asked. "Practical jokers set the Dumpster on fire?"

"How'd you . . . You've already been back there, haven't you? Probably harassing Gordon. How'd you get here from the park?"

"Mom gave me a ride."

"She's here?"

"Just up the road."

The chief shook his head. "Good grief."

"What's Gordon looking for?" I asked.

"Hit the road. We can talk in the morning."

Then it dawned on me why Gordon had been checking the back door. It had probably been jimmied.

"Someone set the fire to get the house evacuated, and then broke in. That's what happened, isn't it? They were looking for Elaine Novak's stuff."

The chief removed his hat, took a deep breath, and ran a hand through his gray crew cut. "Vince, is there something you don't understand about hitting the road?"

"No, but—"

"In the morning, Vince," he said with a note of finality that told me I was on the verge of being hauled off by one of his patrol cops, or maybe one of the firefighters milling around. "In the morning."

Mom's car was in the same spot when I returned. I pulled open the passenger door and climbed in.

"Was anyone hurt?" she asked.

"No. It was a Dumpster fire. No damage to the house from what I could tell."

I glanced into the backseat. Mom had covered Glory with a blanket, and my daughter looked peaceful.

"What about Elaine?"

"She was staying there but left today."

Mom started the engine and turned the car around.

"I think the fire was a diversion, and someone broke into the house after everyone left. At least that's what I assume from what little Gordon and the chief told me. They both seemed a little ticked off to see me."

"No doubt they were," Mom said.

"Huh?"

"Vince, you can be a royal pain in the patootie sometimes."

"Thanks for your support."

We rode in silence for a few moments, Mom navigating back through the downtown area before heading north to our home. A little less than a year ago, when we'd had a short-term falling-out and talking had been hard, silences like this were even harder. And a comment like "Thanks for your support" wouldn't have been accepted as a joke.

Since that time we've become closer, and I knew Mom was thinking of the best way to set me straight.

"What would you think, Vince, if Dale showed up at the newspaper one morning, stood looking over your shoulder, and asked you questions about why you were using the words you used? Or what if Gordon tagged along on an interview and kept interrupting when you were trying to do your job?"

"It's not quite the same, Mom."

"In your mind it's not. But how about from their perspective?"

She turned onto the lakeshore road. The moon, nearly full, laid a platinum path on Superior and bathed the trees and road with a gray-white light that seemed to turn the world monochromatic. Offshore, the silhouette of an ore carrier headed out of Apostle Bay.

Mom looked over at me. "Vince, let Dale do his job. You know how proud he is of this town. To have these problems—the judge's death, the strife at city hall—he takes it personally. I know you're trying to help, but Dale sees it more like you don't trust him to do his job. Do you understand?"

"Yeah, I guess I do. But a lot of what happens is beyond his control."

"That's exactly my point. He likes having control. He prides himself on it."

Mom pulled into our driveway and stopped.

"Are you and the chief dating, Mom?"

She laughed. "Dating? My goodness, I haven't heard that term in a long time."

"It's just I've noticed you don't call him the chief anymore. You call him Dale."

"Good night, Vince," she said.

"G'night, Mom."

I popped Glory's car seat free and carried her to the house. She was deep in dreamland, and as I climbed the porch steps, I realized I was ready for a visit there myself.

Instead, I heard voices when we came through the front door, and in our kitchen I found Deb, Sarah Dodge, and Elaine Novak sitting at the table.

Chapter Thirty-three

"Vince, where were you?"

Deb rose from the table and came over to check on Glory, still snoozing in her car seat. I lowered our toddler to the floor. Deb unbuckled her and started working her free.

"Didn't you get my note? We caught a ride with Mom."

"That's what I thought, but when you weren't here. . . ."

"We took a detour by the women's shelter," I said, and I glanced toward Sarah and Elaine. "There was a fire."

Elaine gasped and reached for Sarah's arm. Sarah looked exhausted—a rare sight, as most of the time she was rushing off to her next meeting or taking charge of something. She closed her eyes for a moment, as if gathering strength.

"Nothing major," I said. "A Dumpster fire. There was no damage to the house, and no one was injured."

"Thank God," Elaine said.

Sarah opened her gray-blue eyes and looked directly at me, her gaze asking what else I knew.

"It could have just been a prank," I answered.

She nodded; it was slight, just a little dip of her head, telling me she understood I thought it was more.

Elaine, whom I'd only seen working in the clerk's office and had never met, looked at me expectantly, as if I had more to share. I'd thought she was younger from the times I'd seen her in the courthouse, but seeing her close up, I'd guess she was the same as Deb and I, early thirties. She wore an overly large gray hoodie that hid her shape, and she shrank farther inside it when I met her gaze. Her cropped, bleached-blond hair, the dark roots starting to show, was held back with two barrettes, and her large-frame oval glasses seemed more like something to hide behind than a fashion statement.

A carafe of coffee or tea was on the table along with three mugs that seemed untouched.

"Hi," I said. I pulled off my jacket. "I'm Vince. Please excuse my face; I don't always look this hideous."

"We've seen women who look worse, thanks to their husbands or boyfriends," Sarah said.

Ouch. Sometimes Sarah had a way of making me feel guilty for being a man.

Deb touched my arm. "I'm going to put Glory into bed," she said.

I nodded. As she left, I went to the cupboard, grabbed another mug, and sat at the table.

"I've seen you in the clerk's office," I said to Elaine. "And sorry, I didn't mean to shock you. I should have said Dumpster fire in the first place. I understand you were staying at the shelter until today."

A look of concern crossed her face, and she turned to Sarah.

"How'd you know that?" Sarah demanded.

"The cops."

"Which one? They know they can't share that information."

"Whoa, Sarah. Deb had guessed Elaine might be there. I just asked a buddy if she was okay after the fire. He said she wasn't staying there anymore. That's all."

"They have to respect the confidentiality of those women," Sarah said.

"Yeah, but—"

"No buts," Sarah said. "What if her abuser was a firefighter, or a cop, or a newspaper reporter, and that person could find out if she was residing there because he had a buddy on the force?"

I poured from the carafe into my mug. It was coffee, and steam drifted up as the dark liquid splashed in. I hoped it was decaf, as I still planned to catch a little sleep tonight. Both women declined my offer to fill their mugs.

"Deb told me you were looking for Elaine," Sarah said.

"Yeah. Rhonda's been worried about you."

She nodded. "I'm sorry," she said. "I should have called her."

"Don't be sorry," Sarah snapped. I think she realized how harsh she sounded, because then she reached over, patted Elaine's forearm, and smiled. "You were smart to leave home and stay away from the courthouse."

I sipped the Java and waited.

"You know her ex was released," Sarah said. "He made quick time of letting her know."

"Rhonda told me. He sounds like a piece of work."

"He is," Sarah said.

"Did . . . did he do that to your face?" Elaine asked. Her voice quavered. She'd taken her empty mug and started fiddling with the handle.

"I'm not sure. The cops think it might have been someone

else. I did get whacked at your house, though. Did Deb tell you about it?"

"Yeah," Sarah said. "Why do they think it was someone else?"

"It's a long story."

Sarah snorted. "I have no doubt he was involved some-how," she said. "Now you know why Elaine's not staying at home and why she won't be until he's back in jail. He used to do that to her," she said, pointing toward my face. "But he did it in places where no one else could see. She went to the shelter when she heard about the judge, thinking Reggie might have killed him. Today we moved her elsewhere, fig-uring sooner or later Reggie would check the safe house. Sounds like she was just in time. Now you see why it royally ticks me off that the cops told you?"

"I'm sorry."

"How bad was it?" Elaine asked. "My apartment?"

"We haven't had a chance to go there yet," Sarah added.

I sipped, taking a moment to recall the scene. "I don't re-member much. I wasn't thinking too clearly at the time. Mostly it was a mess. Someone had pulled everything out of the cupboards and dumped the contents onto the floor. The kitchen table was overturned. I don't think any major things were broken, but I only saw the kitchen and part of the hall-way before someone popped me."

I'd been watching my mug as I said this. I looked up and caught Elaine staring at me. She turned away, embarrassed.

"Looks that bad, huh?" I cracked a smile, and it hurt.

Sarah muttered under her breath, and I'm pretty sure I caught a curse word.

Deb entered and sat in the fourth chair. "Glory's wiped," she said. "She didn't stir while I changed her and put her down."

"It was a long day for the little whippersnapper," I said.

"Can I get you anything?" Deb asked the two women. They both shook their heads no again.

"Did you talk her into it?" Deb asked.

"What?" Sarah and I said simultaneously.

"Running for judge."

"No," I said. "That was your job."

"Save your breath," Sarah said. "I'm not interested."

"If you don't, we're stuck with either Rudy Clark or Speed Demon Freeman," I said. "And you'll have to deal with them every time you go into court."

"Someone else will run. They're just waiting until the judge is in the ground."

"We could use a woman judge," Deb said.

"That's probably not what most people around here think," Sarah said. "And if that's why you lured us here, you've wasted all our time."

I sipped my coffee again, trying to reorient my thoughts back to the judge. "Actually, I was hoping to ask Elaine about the research she was helping Judge Sorenson do."

"She won't talk to you for the newspaper," Sarah said.

"Sure," I answered, holding my hands up in mock surrender. "It's not an interview."

"I'm here as her attorney too. Are you clear on that?"

"Hey, back off, Sarah. I'm just trying to figure out what happened to the judge and maybe help out Monty Haver. He seems to be the number one suspect right now."

"But the judge was trying to help Monty," Elaine said, her voice light, feathery.

"I guess Monty didn't see it that way. Wasn't there a big blowup between the two?"

Elaine nodded. "Monty wouldn't let the judge explain."

"Explain what?"

Elaine looked down and fiddled with her mug again. Sarah looked ready to pounce at me if I said the wrong thing.

Deb broke the tension. "Vince, why don't you tell them what you told me? Then Sarah and Elaine can decide if there's any way they can help or not."

"Sure," I said.

I explained about my meeting with Patrice, how she'd mentioned the judge's research and how he'd told her it might stop the development. I also explained how I'd learned the cops hadn't been able to find any of the judge's handwritten notes, the original Sorenson journals, or the laptop with the typed notes. I added details about the cemetery vandalism, the strange rumor about money hidden in a coffin, and how the cops caught Monty searching the judge's office, the final item drawing surprised looks from both women.

"I see it this way: one—Monty's behavior seems way out of character, and maybe the judge's notes and stuff will explain why; and, two—someone's making a serious effort to find those notes and journals, and Monty seems like a suspect. The person or persons robbed the judge's house the night of his death and trashed your place—I think trying to find them. I'd be willing to bet they set the Dumpster at the shelter on fire as a diversion tonight and then broke in and searched the building, thinking you had the stuff there."

Sarah didn't blink. I noticed Elaine shrink farther into her sweatshirt.

"If that's true, I'll bet they did it tonight because so many people were at the vigil," Deb said. She paused a moment, then added, "But that rules out Jack Reynolds." The disappointment was clear in her voice.

"I know, and about half the town. I didn't see Monty at the park, though. And they're the only two I know of who have a reason to get their hands on those journals. And maybe judge's nephew, but he was with you too. By the way, how did it go?"

"It was okay," Deb said. "Jack wormed his way back in, but at least he kept his mouth shut. For the most part it was subdued. I think it really hit everyone once we were at the site where, you know . . ."

A small whimper escaped from Elaine, and I noticed tears sliding down her cheeks. She wiped them with one sleeve.

Deb reached across and touched her arm, lingering a moment, then stood and grabbed a box of tissues from the counter.

Elaine wiped her tears and twisted her sweatshirt. Deb pulled her chair closer and put an arm around the woman. Sarah glared at me. Only the hum of our refrigerator broke the silence, and the whisper of Elaine pulling another tissue from the box.

I broke it first. "I figure that the judge hid the stuff, and either Elaine has it, or the judge's nephew does."

"She has all of it," Sarah said.

"The journals, the notes, and the laptop?"

"Yes."

"The judge would never have given it to Peter," Elaine said.

"Why not?"

"The judge couldn't stand him. He said Peter was just here to try to get money."

"Get money? Really?"

"Yes. The judge said his nephew needed money for some investment. He'd asked the judge for it last spring, and Judge

Sorenson told him no. But Peter wouldn't give up. He moved in with the judge last month and kept complaining about how the judge was giving all his money away and that he should look out for family first."

"I wonder if the chief or Gordon know about that. Especially since Peter inherits from the judge. That gives him motive."

"He doesn't," Elaine said.

"He doesn't what?"

"Inherit," Elaine said. "The judge didn't have any children. So he told me that everything he owned went into a foundation, and a board of trustees would decide how to use it for the community."

"That's not what Peter thinks," I said. "The judge wouldn't change that because he was angry about the Explorer's Park thing, would he?"

Elaine shrugged her shoulders. "I don't trust Peter," she said.

"Or Reggie," Sarah said. "He'd already threatened the judge."

"Yeah, Rhonda told me. I think he's on the chief's list."

Sarah looked at her watch, stood abruptly, and said, "We've got to get going."

Elaine seemed surprised, but she stood also.

"Thanks for the coffee," Sarah added.

I thought about mentioning that she hadn't even poured herself a mug.

"Thanks for coming tonight," Deb said. She handed the box of tissues to Elaine. "Here, take this with you."

"No thanks," she said. "I'm fine now."

"Um, what about the journals and laptop?" I asked.

"What about them?" Sarah asked.

"May I look through the stuff?"

She gave me a disapproving look. "You just told us it's evidence in a murder—"

"A possible murder," I interrupted.

"It's evidence. We'll turn it over to the city cops tomorrow."

"But—" Elaine said.

Sarah interrupted her. "We have to. Tomorrow."

"The chief will be happy," I said, hoping that I'd added enough sarcasm to make my point.

Sarah snorted.

Deb hugged Elaine again and then guided them to the door. I followed, wondering if Gord would give me a peek tomorrow morning, although that seemed rather hopeless, considering his and the chief's comments tonight and my ban from the police station.

Sarah opened the door. Elaine hesitated, looking back toward the kitchen. Sarah took her by the arm. "It's okay Elaine," she said.

"But—"

"It's okay," Sarah said again.

Elaine nodded, thanked us again, and followed Sarah out. Deb and I stepped onto the porch. The moon was lower now and throwing its ghostly light through the trees. There was a bite in the air. I put a hand on Deb's back and felt her warmth as we watched Sarah and Elaine climb into Sarah's car and drive away. I couldn't help feeling I'd been close to some important information, and it had slipped through my grasp.

We turned and went back inside.

In the kitchen, Deb started cleaning the table, and I helped, bringing the carafe to the sink and rinsing it. Deb stepped to our sliding glass door for another look at the moon. The little sitting area was still filled with SCALD protest signs, stacks of flyers, and other protest paraphernalia. She started to clear one of the wicker chairs we'd brought in from the porch to use and stopped.

"Sarah must have forgotten this box," she said.

"Huh?"

"She brought this box in when she came," Deb said. "I thought it was SCALD stuff, but it looks like some legal pads with notes. Must be work stuff."

"Let me see that," I said, recalling now the way she'd interrupted Elaine, and hoping the look I'd seen wasn't just imagined. I went over and lifted the box. It was heavy, too heavy for just legal pads.

The legal pads were covered with scribbles that I knew weren't Sarah's handwriting. I lifted them out, setting them on the table, and beneath them I saw what appeared to be small rectangular squares wrapped inside oilcloth and stored inside large Ziploc bags. Beneath those was a laptop computer. My hands felt numb as I lifted the plastic bags out and spread them on the table, silently thanking Sarah, understanding that she'd done this as a favor.

I gently removed the first package from the plastic bag and then opened the tawny oilcloth to find a leather-bound journal. Inside the cover was written:

Journal of Randolph Sorenson: January 14, 1847,
to March 21, 1848

"Better put some more coffee on," I said to Deb. "It's going to be another all-nighter for me."

Chapter Thirty-four

The first journal's leather spine crackled when I opened it. Inside, the pages were yellow and brittle and had the thick, slightly rough texture of vellum. The handwriting, though the ink was faded to a brownish purple, was meticulous and fluid.

Deb stood at my shoulder, watching as I removed the protective cloth from the other three journals. They covered a period of seven years from 1847 to 1854, up to the year Melvin Haver committed suicide.

"Do you think they're really Randolph Sorenson's diaries?" she asked.

"Patrice thought they were genuine."

I carefully fingered through the pages of the first one, remembering Patrice Berklee's admonishment about oils on fingers that caused manuscript deterioration. Feeling guilty, I wiped my hands on my pants, then, realizing that was foolish, went to the sink and washed them. It was an equally silly gesture, but it relieved some of my guilt.

"It's hard to believe these were written by someone who

stood here more than a hundred and fifty years before us," Deb said.

"I know. You want to help me go through them? I think we've only got tonight."

"There's no way you could stop me."

"I'll start at the beginning. How about you start with the last book?" I said, handing her the final diary of the sequence.

"And we'll meet in the middle?"

"Works for me," I said.

I opened the first book and started reading.

January 14, 1847—Messrs. Richard Gilman and Thomas Wharton of Boston Properties LIC have, after much debate and examination of the mineralogical reports received of late, agreed to finance the expedition to the Michigan region, west of Sault Ste. Marie. If the reports are to be believed, copper boulders as big as livestock and iron deposits that set the compass to dancing wait for us there. I can only hope the delay has not been too costly and that we can still win the race to this discovery.

The next several entries detailed Sorenson's planning for the trip, including equipment and supplies he purchased.

February 23, 1847—Mr. Wharton signed the purchase for the Lexington sawmill today. I will ride there tomorrow to supervise the dismantling of the equipment and preparation of the shipment to Sault Ste. Marie. . . .

Through the spring of 1847 Sorenson purchased boilers and food and equipment needed for mining, timber cutting, road building, and ore processing. I read urgency in the tone of his entries, and a frustration with the oversight and pace of his financiers. An entry in June seemed almost despondent.

> *June 10, 1847—Have learned through Masters in De-troit that the Cumberland Mining Company passed through Sault Ste. Marie last fall (two months after I first told Gilman and Wharton we must go!) and has pur-chased large tracts from the U.S. Government land office in Sault. I fear our propensity to study and plan and de-bate rather than seize this opportunity has cost us dearly and can only hope they have left us some land with value.*

Sorenson left by train the following day and boarded the steamer *Huron* in Buffalo two days later. He was joined by his advance man, James Masters, in Detroit.

> *June 15, 1847—Masters has assembled a crew, and we leave on the* Penobscot *in the morning for Sault Ste. Marie. With luck we can still buy land and procure a guide and workers there. We are told only two steamers operate on Lake Superior, and the Cumberland Mining Co. has booked them both for the summer. Cumberland has already sent blooms to Pittsburgh—they have beaten us to the prize and must already have their forge in operation. . . . Trappers at the dock here wear chunks of copper as jewelry and say it tumbles in the streams and can be picked from the roots of trees that have top-pled in the wind.*

The next several pages dealt with the sights of their travel up the Saint Clair River into Lake Huron, including a stop at

Mackinac Island, where the *Penobscot* was waylaid for several days by abysmal weather. I found the first reference to Melvin Haver when Sorenson described his plan to go overland and arrive at Sault Ste. Marie ahead of the other agents, thereby gaining advantage at the land office. His guide was a young boy who claimed to know the route.

June 19, 1847— . . . So much for all the hardened men here at this northern outpost, who appear to be long on tales and short on action. I can find only Melvin Haver, a mere boy of fourteen, stout of heart though slight of build, who is willing to venture north in this miserable weather. He seems to believe himself immortal after surviving the wreck of the Enoch *in the nearby Straits of Mackinac, a tragedy that took his parents. If his bold claims of knowing the trail to Sault Ste. Marie are true, we may gain advantage yet.*

June 21, 1847—We have arrived in Sault after crossing what I can only term as the most miserable, Godforsaken wilderness that must exist on this continent. Rain has been continuous and driving and the wind howling so I had to put my lips to the boy's ear and shout to be heard. He informs me I should be grateful for the weather, as it has kept the mosquitoes and blackflies at bay. I don't know if I agree but am obliged as weather has also delayed the Penobscot.

I have engaged the boy Haver, who seems indefatigable, to spend the night lying at the door of the land office so I may be first through it tomorrow. For the sum of a dollar he has agreed to defend his post with honor.

Sorenson wrote that he found lodging in a private home in Sault Ste. Marie owned by fur trapper John Marbury and Marbury's Ojibwa wife, Betty. After food and a warm bath it appears he questioned Marbury at length about the Cumberland holdings and land west of Pictured Rocks. He proposed to hire Marbury as a guide.

After reading further I realized Patrice was right about Randolph Sorenson's being a gambler. He staked everything on advice Marbury had offered.

June 22, 1847—I arrived at the land office today in time to observe a scene of utter chaos. True to his word, the boy Haver had not allowed any man to enter the building, including the superintendent, who had called upon officers from Fort Brady to dispatch what he believed was an impudent whelp gone mad. They had young Haver immobilized and were discussing his disposition when I was able to explain the misunderstanding and mollify the superintendent with a gift. . . .

. . . I saw on the superintendent's map what Marbury had so aptly explained as Cumberland's error in judgment. While they had purchased great swaths of land where iron seems most abundant, they neglected to buy land at the harbor proper. Indeed, their only holding is a small parcel at the mouth of the Silver River, where Marbury said their forge lies about a mile upstream. If Marbury is to be believed, the coast at the Silver is unsuitable for shipping, as it is directly exposed to the north wind and also treacherous with submerged rock.

. . . have decided after studying the land holdings, our fortune lies not in the minerals but in controlling passage out of this wilderness. With the letter of credit from

Boston Properties I purchased most of the lakeshore in a protected bay north and west of the Silver River. Also, to satisfy Messrs. Gilman and Wharton, I purchased land north and west of the bay, which Marbury assures me will provide minerals and timber for construction of the town and shipping pier. The cost was $356. I purchased additional shoreline and timberland for myself also upon Marbury's advice. The cost was $72.

The next entries showed that Sorenson assembled an expedition team to leave immediately to explore his purchases. They would travel by canoe. His team consisted of Marbury, who would guide them; two fellow trappers willing to paddle for pay; a Jesuit priest named Father Benoit, who had agreed to serve as interpreter to the Ojibwa (Sorenson seemed to think the priest had other reasons for leaving town expeditiously— something to do with his bar tab at a local tavern); a state land surveyor who'd been left behind by his team to battle food poisoning and hoped to catch up with them; five men who signed on as laborers; and Haver.

He left word for James Masters that he had gone ahead to survey the land purchase and construct a dock for receiving the equipment and machinery, and that Masters should as soon as possible unload and haul the equipment up the St. Mary's River portage. Since the Cumberland Mining Company had a stranglehold on the two steamers plying the lake, Sorenson cut a deal with the captain of the schooner *Odawa* to drag his ship up the portage and transport the equipment and men west.

The next several days provided descriptions of their travel and the scenery, intermingled with Sorenson's evolving and somewhat grandiose plans to build a port city and control the region's shipping. In some passages he also shed light on

Marbury's motivation—mainly being an act of revenge against the Cumberland Mining Company for refusing to pay for some service he had rendered them.

June 24, 1847—Left Sault this A.M. For the first time in a week the sky is clear and water calm. Canoes moved swiftly. . . .

June 26, 1847—Spent the day paddling at the face of towering bluffs that rise from the lake in a perpendicular manner to great heights, stratified with a spectrum of vivid color from the discharge of minerals as if a canvas painted upon by an ancient Titan or, as Father Benoit assures us, by the hand of God. The immensity and grandeur left me thinking there must be some way to capitalize on this natural creation.

June 27, 1847— . . . caught in storm and forced to remain ashore . . . Marbury tells me we could see our destination from here in clear weather and suggests we continue on by land. Marbury and I will set out on foot while the rest follow when the lake calms. . . . I cannot spend yet another night with the insufferable priest. . . . He should pray that the others do not test his ability to walk on water during the final leg of their voyage.

June 28, 1847—Arrived today after a short detour up the Silver River to reconnoiter the Cumberland forge. I am convinced Marbury was correct. Cumberland erred in its judgment of a site. The bay we own is protected by natural geology. . . .

Chapter Thirty-five

I stopped at this point, needing to stretch my back and legs. I'd been so engrossed that I forgot to refill my mug with the coffee I'd brewed an hour earlier.

Deb had her nose buried inside the last journal.

"Finding anything interesting?" I asked.

"Oh, yeah. This is fascinating."

"Anything about Sorenson's giving the land to Melvin Haver?"

"No," she said. "Nothing like that. But—just let me finish. This explains a lot."

I watched her read a bit more, and it reminded me of when we'd studied together in college, Deb reviewing the material with a quiet intensity, me studying the way her brown hair hung around her face as she leaned on one elbow, or the way her fingers, long and supple, held her pen when taking notes—which explains why she received much better grades than I.

I went back to Sorenson's journal, this time skimming more of the passages. Time was against us.

The general summary was that James Masters arrived the week after Sorenson's expedition, and, using the equipment he'd brought, built a receiving dock, a road, and lodgings. Over the next few months additional equipment arrived. The explorers cobbled together a port, and a town began to take shape.

Sprinkled throughout the diary were references to "the boy Haver" and the things he did for the group, from diving into Superior's frigid water to retrieve tools, to hunting and fishing for food, to helping construct a post office–general store, to operating the sawmill.

Sorenson eventually stopped referring to Haver as "the boy" and called him Haver and then, later, Mel.

There were also passages about the town's name, and I learned that Apostle Bay wasn't the first choice.

July 3, 1847—There has been much debate about what to call the town that is now rising out of this wilderness. Masters votes for New Boston. Marbury insists we use some Indian name I can't pronounce. Haver recommended Sorenson City. That insufferable priest, who seems all too happy to share our provisions but not our labor, has been calling this place Apostle Bay. He claims the twelve men in our expedition were as divinely guided as the original twelve—he being the divine guide, I think. I have decided to call our town Independence.

July 17, 1847— . . . received a third shipment on the Odawa *today . . . the ship's captain refers to us as*

Apostle Bay. Benoit is the cause. He greets all arrivals despite my efforts . . . I will send a letter with the next shipment to the superintendent of the land office in Sault explaining our correct name is Independence.

I'm not sure when Sorenson eventually gave up the battle, but by September even he was referring to the town as Apostle Bay in his journal.

Throughout his entries Sorenson also seemed to waffle on his relationship with Boston Properties. He often expressed frustration that they did not move fast enough or provide enough quality materials, sending instead remanufactured items and equipment. He often railed at the control they exerted over his decisions and profits.

The journal also tells that he turned over some of the business management to Haver, such as running the general store and ordering supplies.

In October, Sorenson left on the *Odawa* and returned to Sault Ste. Marie, where he bought more land and met an incoming load of equipment. He also took shipment of goods he hoped would help the town survive the winter.

But his main reason for traveling to the Sault was to meet with the special agent of the U.S. Postal Service and receive approval to run a post office from the Apostle Bay general store. The current post office was in New Cumberland, the small settlement on the Silver River near the Cumberland Mining Company forge.

Sorenson was convinced that his competitor was both tampering with and destroying his mail.

In order to convince the special agent there was merit to an added post office, he bribed the postmaster in Sault to fill empty mail bags with junk and label them for Apostle Bay.

Sorenson's plan paid off, and the town soon had a functioning post office. The first postmaster of Apostle Bay was Melvin Haver.

Sorenson's first major break came in late October of that same year when the steamer *Ithaca* tore its hull on rocks near the mouth of the Silver River. That cut Cumberland Mining Company's shipping capacity in half and resulted in the captain of the other steamer, the *Henry Lee,* insisting on receiving loads only at the protected Boston Properties dock.

The second piece of fortune for Sorenson and crew came in the spring after a devastating winter nearly wiped out the settlement as supplies ran short. During spring melt-off the Silver River flooded and destroyed Cumberland's forge and part of its settlement. When the shipping season reopened and Boston Properties got its first steamer past the St. Mary's River, Sorenson controlled the shipping and the port and had the only working forge in the region, gravitas he leveraged into further growth and land purchases.

Within another year Cumberland Mining sold its entire Upper Peninsula venture.

Ironically, when Cumberland abandoned its settlement and the postmaster left, Haver was promoted to postmaster of New Cumberland. The U.S. Postal Service believed New Cumberland was the center of town and Apostle Bay was an outlying community, rather than the other way around.

I heard Deb close her journal, so I leaned back, grabbed my mug, and took a swig, even though I knew it'd gone cold by now.

The cracks in our house whistled, the way they do when

the wind is easterly, coming off the lake. Wind from the east usually means a weather change.

Deb shook her head and looked up at me, her eyes red with exhaustion.

"I just don't get it, Vince," she said.

Chapter Thirty-six

Deb went to the sink and filled a glass with water. She said, "This explains a lot—especially the hard feelings between Monty Haver and the judge."

"The profit skimming?" I asked. "By Melvin?"

She nodded. "If this was about my ancestor, I wouldn't want it dredged up again. It's terribly embarrassing. I can see why Monty would be upset."

"Upset enough to try to steal the journals? Maybe to kill the judge?"

She shrugged. "Depends on the type of person he is."

I joined her at the sink, dumped the dregs from my mug, and poured a refill. The window reflected back my puffy bruises.

"Want any?" I asked Deb, holding the pot her way.

"No," she said absently, as if the diary still held her in its grip. She stretched her back and rolled the kinks out of her neck. Her hair was mussed on one side, sticking out the same way Glory's sometimes does when she falls asleep on one arm.

"What I don't understand is why he'd do it," she said.

"Who? Monty?"

"No, Melvin Haver. Sorenson gave him everything. Things were going great. Melvin was managing the business, making money, and had plenty of responsibility. He was married, had two young children. The company provided everything for him. And from what I gather, Sorenson basically adopted him as a kid, raised him, and made him almost a partner in the business."

"Not quite adopted, but he did give the kid his break," I said. I gave her a quick summary of how they met.

"So, in a way, Sorenson was a father figure to Melvin," she said.

"In a way."

"Then why betray him?"

"Greed? Ambition? Money? All of the above?"

"That's what Sorenson wrote. All of the above. And he was bitter about it. I mean, listen to this."

She strode to the table, flipped open the journal, and then paged backward from the end until she reached the passage.

"This was written September 24, 1854. He writes:

Haver's deception wounds me. It is a personal betrayal because of the trust I placed in him. To know that my faith has been repaid with treachery, that I had my own Judas—for he was one of the Apostles, one of the original men I brought with me and for whom I named this town. I understand now I can trust no one.

"So if they're the apostles, and Haver was Judas, who does that make Sorenson?" I asked. "And the town *he* named? Sorenson hated the name Apostle Bay. He tried to change it."

"That's not the point," Deb said. "The point is that Haver stole from his mentor and probably jeopardized the entire operation. In the journal Sorenson tells how at his own expense he repaid the missing funds to keep Boston Properties from pulling its support."

"How did Sorenson find out Melvin Haver was stealing?"

"I got the impression that Sorenson turned over most of the bookkeeping to Melvin because he didn't have the patience for dealing with his financiers, the company's owners."

"Same in the first journal," I said. "He complains they take too long to make decisions. Although, considering the way people communicated back then, it's amazing they were able to get much done at all. And it sure seems like Boston Properties was free with their money for the items he bought. Then again, I can imagine the frustration of waiting for word to travel halfway across the U.S. and back, especially because Sorenson seemed obsessed with the competition."

"Yep, there's some of that too," she said. "Anyway, he's not very clear on how he figured out Melvin was stealing, just that he'd called him on it. He describes it here, in the next entry:

We went to Haver's home and confronted him about his perfidy, this rodent, this deer mouse who has been scurrying behind our walls, collecting, gathering, hoarding, out of sight, with no regard for his benefactors. He offered not a single crumb of shame or regret for his betrayal.

"It really says that?"

Deb cracked her first smile since we'd been sitting at the table. "Yeah. Sounds like a cheesy novel. Lots of clichés and drama. Then again, it's a diary, and he probably wasn't overly concerned with his word choice."

"Does it ever say how much Haver stole?"

"I didn't find a figure anywhere. Only that Sorenson paid it back. Nothing was ever recovered from the Haver family that I could tell."

"Which explains the rumor of buried treasure. Anything else?"

"Just that Sorenson and a guy named Marbury—"

"He shows up in the first diary too—"

"—discovered Haver's body the next day, hanging from a tree outside Haver's house. Sorenson called it a fitting end for a traitor."

"No reference to Melvin Haver's owning the property?"

"None that I found."

"We have a few more hours until daylight. Want to tackle the other two journals?"

"Do we have any good snacks to get me through it?"

"How about some grape Pop-Tarts?" I said.

Deb gave me the "get real" look and said, "I meant something with chocolate in it."

Then she reached for another volume of Sorenson's life.

Chapter Thirty-seven

Lou's *Lone Ranger* ring tone woke me the next morning.

When the music stopped, I sought return to a place where the pain in my face wasn't real and my daughter's shrieking was part of the dream. I might have found refuge, had I not recalled the previous night and jerked upright, expecting to discover a puddle of drool on one of Randolph Sorenson's 150-year-old journals.

With relief I saw instead a yellow legal pad with the judge's precise handwriting—every letter the same height and width, as if he'd used a template. I recalled that we'd packed the journals back into their oilcloth and plastic bags before Deb headed off to bed, while I tried to browse the judge's notes.

It was still dark outside. The kitchen clock showed 6:03. I'd snagged about an hour's rest.

I blinked away sleep, working my eyes farther open with each attempt. My tongue, dried from breathing through my mouth all night, thanks to crushed nasal passages, felt swollen and rough.

I pushed myself away from the table, went to the sink to splash water on my face, then stumbled down the hall to get Glory, hoping Deb could snooze another half hour before she had to rise for work.

No longer shrieking, Glory held her crib rail and played trampoline. I scooped her out and moved straight to the changing table. The cell sang again from my pocket. I flipped it open, hit the speaker, and set it down by the diaper wipes.

"Mornin', Lou,"

"Are you on or off today, Vince? Ah, doesn't matter. Mort and Ashley are overloaded, and I don't have anyone to cover a fire at the women's shelter last night. Make some calls, and get me something for today on it."

The fire seemed like days ago, not hours ago. I unzipped Glory's sleeper and started working her feet out. She was trying to sit up and grab the phone. I held her chest down with my right arm and stretched the jammies foot over her toes.

"I have it covered, Lou. It was a Dumpster fire."

"Give me a brief, then."

"There could be more to it. Last night the cops seemed to think the fire might have been a diversion for a break-in."

"I don't suppose you have art?"

"I'll e-mail it within a half hour."

"Sooner would be good. And forget the brief. Just put the info into the picture cutline."

"Sure," I said.

"By the way, you're the lead today."

"What? You just said put the info into a cutline."

"Not that. You. Your daughter's kidnapping. The burglar you ran into. That whole fiasco. Ashley got a nice photo of your face. You really took it on the chin, didn't you?"

"Lou, you can't use that."

"It's a good story. I'm starting to like this girl."

"Great," I said. "And to answer your first question: I'm off today."

"Glad to hear it. Then send me that art, but don't put it on your time sheet." He hung up.

While I packed away Glory's diaper, she escaped from her sleeper and started over the table's side. I snagged her and, between playful kicks, cleaned her and installed another diaper.

"Mama!" Glory said.

"Who was that?" Deb asked through a yawn. She stood in the doorway, hair disheveled, still wearing her clothes from last night.

"Who do you think?"

"You didn't agree to go in, did you?"

"No, I certainly didn't. Not after he told me he's plastering a photo of my swollen face on page one today. I can't believe Ashley did that to me."

I set Glory on the floor, and she tumbled across the room to hug Deb.

"On the front page?"

"Hopefully no one will recognize me."

"Fat chance. Well, at least yesterday your bruises were purple. Today they're the color of baby poop."

"That makes me feel a whole lot better."

Deb grinned. "By the way, did you find anything else? Anything in the judge's notes?"

We'd finished browsing the journals early this morning before Deb slipped off to bed. She'd found the passage—a short sentence—where Sorenson described giving Haver a parcel for his wedding. It was brief on details and wouldn't have meant anything unless you knew that Haver built his homestead on the north side of the Manitou River, near the existing monument.

The vague reference disappointed Deb, and she'd given up at that point.

"Nada," I said. "But I didn't last too long after you left."

Deb went to shower and get ready for school. I tossed Glory onto the couch, flipped on PBS, then went into the kitchen and turned on my computer. While it booted, I brewed a new pot of coffee and called Gord to see what he'd tell me about the fire.

The detective was out. I decided I'd try him again after breakfast rather than knock heads with my godfather. I wasn't in the mood for another lecture.

I mixed a packet of instant oatmeal, popped it into the microwave, and, while it cooked, downloaded the pictures from my camera. Then I set up Glory's booster seat, cleared a space for her oatmeal and some juice, and snagged her from the living room couch.

"Oatmeal okay?" I called to Deb.

"No time!" she yelled back. "I'll grab something on the way."

Back in the kitchen I strapped in Glory, cleared all the Sorenson materials from the spill zone, and then gulped a mouthful of Java.

"What were you watching?"

"Tubby-tubbies," she said.

"How have we degenerated from Mozart in utero to Tipsy-Wipsy?"

I'd strung over the phone line while saying this and plugged in. While the modem dialed, I banged out a photo cutline.

"Tinky-Winky," she said.

"Right."

I sent the e-mail. As the progress bar went across my screen, a wad of goop splattered it.

"Glory!"

"Time for Tubby bye-bye," she said, giggling.

The doorbell saved her.

I passed Deb on her way into the kitchen as I went to answer it.

"I don't have time for anyone," she said, grabbing her coat and briefcase. She spun by Glory, kissed her head, and went through the kitchen door into the garage.

I saw Gord through the front window and swung the door open.

"Come in, bud," I said, heading back to the kitchen to make sure no more oatmeal was flying. "You're just the guy I wanted to see."

Glory had finished her oatmeal, unbuckled, and was climbing from the booster. I didn't see signs of other splotches. She slapped Gordon a high five on her way back to the land of the brain-dead while I grabbed Gord a mug.

"Coffee?"

"Sure."

I poured him a cup and set it on the table.

"Did you get my message? Decide to answer it in person?"

"Huh?"

"I called earlier. To get more details about last night's fire."

"You're not even working today."

"I am from home," I said, pointing at the computer. The oatmeal glob had slid down the monitor and onto the keyboard. I moved it to the counter, grabbed a napkin, and tried to clean it, cursing under my breath since I knew I'd never get the stuff out of the crevices.

A deep vibration rumbled through the wall.

"The garage door," I said, in answer to Gord's raised eyebrow. "You missed Deb. She's on her way to work."

Had we not been friends since high school, I probably wouldn't have noticed the slight change in Gord when I said that: the way his easygoing grin froze, the way he shifted forward onto the balls of his feet, and the way his eyes narrowed their focus, scanning the room. A second later he'd relaxed again, reached over and grabbed the mug I'd set near him, and held it up in a gesture of thanks.

"The fire—what can you tell me?"

"Nothing more than you already know. You'll have to talk with the chief if you want some kind of comment." He sipped. "Good coffee."

"Better than the swill you serve. Was it a B and E?"

He sipped again, and I could see him smile behind the mug.

"Are you going to release any more info before today's deadline?"

"Call the chief," he said.

"Thanks, buddy."

"Anytime."

He took another sip, set the mug on the table, and sidled over to the box Elaine and Sarah had left. He picked up one of the journals.

"Since you obviously didn't come to help me," I asked, "why are you here?"

He waved the journal at me. "I heard you have something I've been looking for."

The thought of denying it crossed my mind, but I realized that the only way he could know was if Sarah had called him. He'd probably tensed a moment earlier because he thought Deb was driving off with them.

"Elaine Novak had that stuff. I think she left it here last night by accident."

"I see. By accident."

"Isn't that what Sarah told you?"

He smiled. "That's what she said, *after* she reamed me for telling you that Elaine had left the shelter. Did you get a chance to look at this stuff?"

"We got through the journals. I'd hoped to look at the judge's notes and laptop this morning."

"Find anything interesting?"

"It's basically what Patrice said it was. Why don't you leave it here for a while and let me finish? I'll bring the whole box down at lunchtime."

He chuckled. "Is everything here?"

"Yeah," I conceded. "The laptop and journals are in the box. The legal pads are on the chair over there," I said, pointing to a wicker patio chair that was holding up some SCALD signs. "Should I come down to the office and help you go through it? There's a lot of material."

"Patrice is going to lend her expertise."

"I see. So I should call her this afternoon."

Gord winked at me and then placed the protected journal back into the box.

I helped him pack the other items and walked him to the door.

"Can you check on my car today? I need my kayak and gear. The class is doing a full-moon paddle tonight, and all that stuff is still with the vehicle."

"I don't think you need to worry," Gord said. "The wind's picking up, and it's supposed to rain most of the day. It'll be canceled."

It did look gloomy out the window, and the thought of going out on the big lake in a cold rain wasn't appealing.

"I could probably use the sleep anyway. But I still need wheels."

"I'll look into it," he said.

"Better yet," I said, getting a wild idea as he stepped out onto our porch, "can you give us a ride into town? I need to run some errands."

"I don't have a car seat," he said.

"No worries, Gord. Ours is back in the kitchen. Give me five minutes to pack Glory's stuff, and I'll be ready to go."

Chapter Thirty-eight

I t took me ten to get ready—not bad, considering I changed clothes, ran a blade across my face, found an old ball cap to shove onto my head, and then packed our toddler-toting backpack with enough stuff for us to survive a day on the go.

Gord was acting like a human swing set for Glory when I returned to the living room.

"Here, take this," I said, handing him the pack. "I'll grab the car seat."

"Man, are you heading into town or off on a three-day trip?" he asked, making a show of how much the pack weighed.

"You'll understand when you're a dad."

Gordon dropped us at the courthouse's side entrance. The sky had turned that foreboding slate gray that makes it hard to sense time. It was spitting too, not quite raining or sprinkling but drips of moisture that almost wanted to be flurries.

"What do you want me to do with the car seat?" he asked.

"Keep it for now. You might need to pick up a young suspect."

"Vince—"

"I'll walk over and get it when I'm through here."

I slipped the backpack over my shoulders, lifted Glory into one arm, and with a wave to Gordon climbed the steps to Monty Haver's office.

Rhonda was behind the clerk's counter helping a young couple fill out a birth certificate request. She excused herself when we came in and met me where the counter was hinged to allow access to the back offices.

"Candle lady," Glory announced.

"Candle girl," Rhonda answered. "Nice shade of greenish yellow around your nose, Vince. Does it still hurt?"

"Only when someone reminds me about it."

"Monty was hoping you'd be here. C'mon through. I'll bring in the coffee when I'm done out here."

She opened the gate, then knocked and opened Monty's door. "Vince is here," she said, then waved us in.

I lowered Glory to the floor and grasped her hand, but she wriggled it free as we entered Monty's office. He leaned on the windowsill behind his massive desk, his white shirt open at the collar. Behind him the horizon looked like a gray, waving curtain. It was raining out on the lake, probably moving this way. The ore dock, a massive concrete and steel structure that rises above the water and defines our harbor, sat empty for the moment, waiting for the next ship to come and collect a load of iron pellets.

"Is this your daughter? I've wondered what she's like," he said, his voice weary. "Does she need to be here?"

"I had limited options this morning," I said. "And Rhonda said you wanted to talk."

Monty sighed, stepped away from the window, and collapsed into his chair.

"I'll set her up over here with some crayons," I said. I balanced the pack next to his conference table, then pulled out a box of crayons and my reporter's notebook. "C'mon, Mornin' Glory, color me a picture."

"No," Glory said. Instead she dug through the pack, tossing all the other contents onto his carpet.

Monty looked our way, but he didn't seem to be watching us. "Close the door," he said.

I closed the door, then came back and sat down in one of the two wooden chairs that faced his desk—the same chair I'd been sitting in a little less than a year ago when Monty had shown me documents that turned my life upside down. This time I got the feeling our roles were reversed.

"Melvin Haver, my great-great-grandfather, was murdered by Randolph Sorenson," he said.

"Come again?"

Monty sighed and, looking up at the ceiling, said, "Of course, no one believes that."

Glory was humming now, and I glanced her way. She'd found a picture book and was flipping the pages.

"I see."

"I suppose you know the popular version of the story— that Melvin hanged himself?"

"Patrice Berklee gave me a brief rundown. And I've read Sorenson's journals."

He snapped forward, coming out of his chair and leaning across the desk. "You have? When? How'd you get them?"

"Elaine Novak had them," I explained. "She left them with me last night."

"They ought to be destroyed," he said. "They're full of lies—I'm sure of it."

"The cops have them now," I said.

Monty dropped back into his chair, deflated.

"Monty? What do you think happened?"

He waved a hand, a gesture saying it wasn't important.

"I'd like to hear it."

"I'd pretty much forgotten it—at least I'd put it out of my mind—until Dexter had to go and stir things up again. After what the Sorensons have done to us, I don't know why he couldn't leave it alone."

Monty's door opened, and Rhonda came in with two steaming mugs.

"Elaine told me the judge was trying to help you, Monty. Not open old wounds."

"If he wanted to help me, he'd have burned those books and left me alone."

Rhonda set the mugs down on Monty's desk and looked first at me, then her boss. "You two look more somber than the weather. What's going on?"

"Grab a seat, Rhonda. It's time for you to hear this too. You may be the only one who'll believe me."

Chapter Thirty-nine

"Melvin's parents died in a shipwreck on the Straits of Mackinac," Monty said, referring to the location where Lake Michigan and Lake Huron meet at the peak of Michigan's Lower Peninsula, a narrow stretch of water now spanned by the Mackinac Bridge. "He was fourteen."

Monty gave a brief summary of his ancestor's life, a tale similar to that told by Sorenson's journals—until the ending.

"Boston Properties suspected Randolph Sorenson was skimming profits from their port operations and taking kickbacks on the various equipment contracts," Monty said. "They sent a private investigator to check it out. That investigator approached my great-great-grandfather because he was closest to Sorenson and to the business operations."

"Sorenson's journals described Melvin as the bookkeeper," I said. "They describe him as handling all the accounts."

"Not true," Haver said. "Sorenson kept a tight rein on the money and handled as much of it himself as possible. And there was a reason for that. If anyone else got too involved, they'd have seen what was going on

"Melvin trusted Sorenson and refused to help in the investigation—until he learned that the company planned to fire his boss. When Melvin heard that, he set out to prove the investigator wrong, to prove Sorenson's innocence. Instead, he found out the man he'd been working for was bilking the company.

"But even with the evidence, Melvin wouldn't betray his mentor," Haver said. "Instead, he confronted him and was murdered for it."

"By Sorenson?"

"Sorenson and some guy named Marbury. They staged it like a suicide and blamed Melvin for the bookkeeping discrepancies, making it sound as if he'd killed himself when he knew he'd been caught."

"Is there any way to prove that?"

"Melvin wasn't stupid," Monty said. "While he wanted to believe Sorenson was innocent, or at least hear his reasons, he also had the evidence. And he knew a lot of money was at stake. So my great-great-grandfather gathered the documents and hid them in a safe place as insurance to protect his family. Melvin explained all this to his wife, Charlotte, the night he was to meet with Sorenson. He told her that he'd hidden the evidence at the general store, afraid that if it was in his home, it would endanger his wife and children.

"That evening he sent his wife and children into town to visit friends, and he confronted Randolph Sorenson. When Charlotte came home, she and the children found him. . . ."

"What did she do?" I asked, picturing again the judge's body swinging from the tree three days ago.

"Charlotte knew what had happened, and she also confronted Sorenson, threatening him with the evidence. But he'd learned about what Melvin had done. And that night, the night Melvin died, the store burned to the ground. It was a total loss, with the added bonus that Sorenson could claim his records had been destroyed. Charlotte had nothing but her husband's word.

"In the end, Charlotte had no choice. For the sake of her children and herself, she kept her mouth shut while Sorenson spread his story that my great-great-grandfather was the criminal. And Sorenson, the self-serving martyr, made restitution to Boston Properties—allegedly to protect Melvin's family from prosecution.

"That's why, even in their graves, my ancestors can't rest. Rumor spread that the money Melvin stole was never recovered—because, of course, it didn't exist. But no one knew that, and soon after his death treasure hunters were digging up the land around his house. They would have torn apart the house itself, if Sorenson hadn't gotten to it first, dismantling it, probably in search of anything that would incriminate him.

"Now it's happening again, thanks to the judge."

"How sad," Rhonda said.

"Sad," echoed Glory, who was now scribbling in my notebook with an orange crayon.

"Did Charlotte give up the river property as part of her deal with Sorenson?" I asked.

"Ha! The dirtbag took that. He'd given it to them as a wedding present. But Charlotte couldn't prove she owned the land. She couldn't find a deed or document and was forced off the property by Sorenson."

"Monty, how do you know all this?"

"It would be better if I didn't," Monty said, sighing again. "We Havers pass the story down each generation, knowing there's nothing we can do about it. I thought it had finally died, become such a part of the past that my grandchildren would never have to hear it or the lies about our family. Instead, the judge had to bring it all back up again." Haver looked from Rhonda to me. "I'm glad he died." Then, as if he'd realized what he said, he added quietly, "But I didn't kill him."

"You have nothing but the story passed down?" I asked.

"My father fooled himself into believing he'd find the proof. He interviewed old folks around town and at Lakeview Elder Care—anyone who knew our family. He had this . . . this belief, I guess you could call it, that Melvin wouldn't have hidden his insurance in the store, that he'd be smarter than that. His theory was that the details got mixed up as the story was passed down and that the evidence might still be hidden somewhere in town. He even went to Dexter's father once and pleaded his case, but the guy tossed him out and threatened to sue for slander. It was a waste of time, really. But it gave my dad hope."

Rhonda walked around Monty's desk and hugged him. The big man didn't move, but I saw in his eyes that he was grateful, and maybe relieved to get this story out.

I took a quick glance at Glory. She was still in the zone.

"Monty, you said you had nothing to do with the judge's death. But have you been trying to obtain the judge's journals?"

"Why?"

"Vince, I don't think this is the time," Rhonda said.

"Someone's been searching for the judge's notes and the journals," I said. "They tossed his house the night he died, they tore through Elaine's apartment, and I think they broke into the women's shelter, believing she might have them there."

"If I could get my hands on those records, Vince, I'd feed them through a shredder. But do you see me breaking into someone's house?"

"You searched the judge's office."

Monty stared at me, seemed to weigh his answer, and then nodded. "I wanted to find that stuff before someone else did," he said.

"You went to his house the night he died."

"I was afraid of what he planned to do. I wanted to ask him again to let it drop."

"Papa?" Glory said.

"I don't understand why anyone else would be searching for those documents. What's the motive? Everything the journals say supports the Sorenson version, not yours. So who would—?"

"Papa," Glory said again.

"Just a moment, Mornin' Glory."

"Didn't Elaine say the judge was trying to help Monty?" Rhonda said.

"Yeah. But she said Monty misunderstood."

Rhonda moved forward and sat on a corner of Monty's desk. "What if Monty's dad hadn't been on a wild goose chase?" she said. "What if there was a way to prove Monty's story, and the judge knew about it? Maybe he even had it."

"What would he gain by giving it to Monty?" I said.

"He wanted to stop the development. Maybe it's related to that."

"Documents proving Monty was the rightful landowner?" I asked.

"Papa," Glory said, a whining tone creeping into her voice.

"How about this?" Rhonda asked. "What if the judge didn't actually have such documents but said he did?"

"Then someone would call him on it," I said.

"Papa!"

"Or someone would try to find and destroy them," Rhonda said.

"Vince," Monty said. He was pointing at Glory. At the same time the smell that had been on the edge of my consciousness hit me, and I turned.

"Poo-poo," my half-naked toddler said, holding a loaded diaper my way.

Chapter Forty

After taking care of Glory's mess, I told Monty I'd try to do something, although I had no idea what. I also made him promise to tell his story to Patrice Berklee that afternoon. If anyone could help him, it was she.

Outside the courthouse I slid Glory into the big, child carrying backpack, and started down the hill toward Sarah Dodge's law office. I wanted to hear Elaine's take on Monty's story, and Sarah could set that up. She owed me for Gordon's early-morning visit.

The wind was coming in off the lake, swirling dust and leaves into tiny tornadoes in the street and bringing the first splatters of a downpour. Glory fussed in the pack, hungry and, I'm sure, tired of being schlepped around. I quick-stepped it the four blocks to keep us as dry as possible.

Sarah's office is an old house halfway between the court and city hall and one block south of our town's main street. When I was growing up in Apostle Bay, we'd called the place Macbeth House. Back then it was black and gray and spooky, with shutters that always seemed to hang crooked. A medieval wrought iron fence, complete with creaking gate, surrounded the property. The place was home to three sisters, retired schoolteachers and most assuredly witches to our preteen minds. Two have since passed on, and the third is now a member of Glory's weekly tea soiree—Deb said she revels in the knowledge that she'd appeared so frightening to us "rapscallions."

When Sarah bought the building, she repainted it a pastel blue with yellow trim. Now she leases the top floor to a seamstress and the basement to a ceramist who can't sell her pottery, so she gives it to Sarah in lieu of rent.

We jogged through the gate and up the walk and almost crashed into Sarah's secretary, who came flying out the door screaming, "Help! Someone help her!"

I swung Glory off my back.

"He's attacking Sarah!" the woman screamed. "Do something!"

"Call 9-1-1," I said, handing her my phone. "And take Glory."

"I've already called," she said. At the same time we heard a siren.

"Take Glory, and get to a safe place!" I shouted.

I bolted up the steps and through the entrance, checking my bearings in the outer office and looking for something to use as a weapon. I heard a crash and a man shouting curses.

"Get down on the floor," Sarah shouted, "or there's more where that came from!"

I heard another crash, shattering pottery, and then a loud grunt.

I grabbed a ceramic bowl off a shelf, figuring I could at least throw it, and then ran through the door into Sarah's office. Chairs lay overturned. Papers and broken pottery littered the floor; a bookshelf had been toppled, books strewn in front of it; the phone lay on the oak floor, the receiver off the hook and beeping.

Sarah stood in a far corner of the room behind the desk, her blouse untucked on one side. Her hair, partway pulled back, had come loose and hung in her face. In her right hand she held a small pepper-spray can aimed toward the ground behind her desk. From that spot came a wheezing sound.

Keeping the bowl ready to throw, I walked around the desk and found a man curled in the fetal position, one hand covering his eyes, the other holding his privates. He wore a familiar-looking plaid work shirt and jeans, and his face around the hand was scarlet.

"Meet Reggie Novak," Sarah said. "I told you he'd screw up and be back in jail soon."

A patrol car arrived soon after, and then Archie Freeman showed up in his bike cop uniform. The officers hauled Reggie away, and as he turned back toward us to scream a curse, I caught my first glimpse of his face and recognized him as the worker who'd been picking through the grave site at the cemetery two days earlier.

I hung in Sarah's conference room with her secretary and Glory while Freeman interviewed Sarah and photographed the scene. Glory remained in the backpack; it's the type that has a stand, and her toes don't quite reach the ground when she's propped in there. She snacked on Cheerios from a plastic bag I'd brought. The whole scene was much better entertainment than *Teletubbies* for her, I'm sure.

Sarah's secretary told me that Reggie Novak had stormed into Sarah's office, demanding to know where Elaine was hiding. Sarah had told her secretary to phone the police and then told Reggie to take a hike. He flipped out.

My best guess as to what happened next was that Sarah maced him. He probably stumbled around the office, still trying to get at her. She'd kicked a field goal between his uprights and sprayed again for good measure.

While we waited for Sarah and Freeman to finish, I called the story in to Lou.

"How fast can you get here?" Lou asked. "I'm almost ready to send down page one."

"The cops won't let me leave, Lou. I'm a witness." I didn't add that I also had my daughter and didn't plan on going in with her again today, or that I was still ticked off that he was going to use my smashed face to sell today's edition. "Besides, it'll be faster if I dictate to Ashley. She'll want to be in on this because I have the feeling it's tied to the judge's death."

"How so?"

"Novak's an ex-con who swore revenge on the judge at his sentencing."

"Well, that's just great," he said. "Ashley already took off for an interview. Mort's on the desk. I'll transfer you and see if I can get the photog over there."

Mort came on the line a few minutes later. "So the sky is falling, and I've got to drop everything and write for you again, eh, Vince? This is getting kind of habit-forming. Maybe I can ghostwrite your memoirs."

"I'm interrupting your snack, aren't I?"

"Yeah. So be quick and good, because I'm sure Lou will ask me if the story's done as soon as I hang up, and then he'll compare it to Ashley's latest masterpiece."

"Did she really do a story about my daughter's brief kidnapping?"

"Oh, yeah," Maki said with a snicker. "You're going to love it. You look just like Rocky at the end of the movie when he's shouting, 'Yo, Adrian!' "

"Lovely," I said.

I gave Mort a rundown and heard him pounding the keyboard while I talked. After I mentioned that Novak could be a suspect in the judge's death, I suggested Maki call the chief for verification.

"Oh, no, can't step on the little princess's toes," he said. "That's her story."

"She's getting your goat, isn't she?"

"You don't know the half of it, 'cause you're never here. She's—"

"I've got to run," I said, interrupting what I knew was going to be a gripe session. "Call me back if you think of anything I missed."

"Sure. By the way, did you know the city has equipment out at Explorer's Park? They're going to start clearing the site tomorrow."

"Already?"

"Oh, yeah. And I need a story for tomorrow. Why don't you give your wife a jingle and see if SCALD wants to protest?"

Archie Freeman kept my interview professional until the *Chronicle*'s photographer showed up, at which point he made some snide comment about how I'd do anything to manufacture news in this town.

Wait until you see today's edition, I thought.

"See why you need to run for judge?" I told Sarah when the door closed behind him.

"Give it up, Vince. He seemed professional enough to me."

My daughter was now roaming free and digging through a

toy box Sarah kept in her conference room. Sarah represented plenty of single moms who couldn't afford child care, so the conference area doubled as a play center.

I gathered Glory's things and kissed the top of her head as she played, thinking it was pretty amazing how well she'd held together so far this morning.

"Let's get out of here and get some lunch, kiddo."

"Sticky bun?" she asked.

"Anything you want."

As I lifted Glory into the backpack, I asked Sarah if she'd arrange another meeting with Elaine.

"I think the judge would want somebody to finish what he'd started," I said. "And she might have information that could help Monty Haver."

"I'll talk it over with her," Sarah said. "Maybe we'll call later this afternoon."

"Thanks. By the way, the city dozers are at Explorer's Park. They're going to start clearing the site tomorrow."

"You're joking," she said.

"That's the rumor. If you're working for SCALD, now might be the time to seek an injunction."

Chapter Forty-one

Sarah offered us a ride to the Laughing Whitefish, but she didn't have a car seat, so Glory and I borrowed her umbrella and hoofed it the three blocks.

The rain fell straight and hard now, no wind. Small creeks flushed both sides of the street. If this kept up, the ground would be too wet for equipment at Explorer's Park.

The usual crowd of retirees sat inside the diner, solving the world's problems. We found Mom in a booth, warming her hands over a cup of tea, and joined her. I ordered a sticky bun and hot chocolate for Glory and a bowl of soup for myself.

Being obtuse, it wasn't until the chief came through the door that I realized Mom had been waiting for someone.

"Sorry, Mom. We'll move to another booth."

"Stay put, Vince. It's not a problem."

The chief reached our table and shot me an annoyed look before turning toward Mom. "Sorry I'm late, Loretta."

"Hi, Chief," Glory said, the words squeaking around her mouthful of bun.

"Have a seat, Chief," I said, and I slid out of the booth. "Glory and I were just moving."

"I can't stay. Something's come up, Loretta. I'm sorry. I just stopped by to see if I could get a rain check."

"Sure," Mom said. "Is everything okay?"

"Everything's fine. I'll, uh, talk to you later."

"Chief, c'mon. Stay, and at least have a cup of coffee with her. Really, we were just keeping your seat warm."

"Can't," he said. "But, Vince, you saved me a trip. Walk me out."

I winked and stage-whispered to Glory, "I'm in trouble now."

Outside we stood under the cafe's awning. Rain drummed the fabric.

"You know what GHB is, Vince?"

"Someone's initials?"

"It's gamma hydroxybutyrate. The street name is Liquid Ecstasy. It's a date-rape drug—colorless, odorless, and if someone slips a dose into your drink, it'll knock you out. Ingest enough, and it'll kill you."

"O-o-o-kay. And you're giving me this chemistry lesson, why?"

"We found a bottle of it in your car."

"Where?"

"In your cup holder."

"Well, it's not mine," I said. "I didn't even know what the stuff was until now. And I wouldn't know where to buy it even if I wanted to."

Up until this point the chief had been looking out toward the street, but now he turned and focused on me.

"I also got the ME's report on the judge today."

"Let me guess. Toxicology showed GHB in his system."

The chief put a hand on my shoulder, and as always when he was trying to slip into the godfatherly role with me, it seemed awkward, stiff.

"Catch a ride home with your mother after lunch."

"How'd you know—?"

"Gordon told me how you got to town. It's time to go home. I need you to lay low for a few days and not muck things up."

Chapter Forty-two

I spent the afternoon at home with Glory *not mucking things up,* whatever that was supposed to mean. We flipped through picture books, watched a DVD, and actually ate some nutritious food. I bathed Glory and, after learning that the kayak outing had indeed been canceled, grabbed a quick shower myself. We both caught a long nap.

Deb woke us when she arrived home that afternoon.

"How was your day?" she asked.

"Just dandy," I said. "We learned about an unsolved, 150-year-old murder, broke up a felonious assault, discovered that the murder weapon used to kill Judge Sorenson was in my car, and were told to stay home and stop mucking things up. Oh, and we learned that the city plans to bulldoze Explorer's Park tomorrow. How was yours?"

Deb studied me a moment, and then said, "Pretty boring in comparison."

We followed her into the bedroom, and I summarized the

day while she changed clothes and Glory did gymnastics on our bed.

"I know what you're thinking, Deb. I shouldn't have been hauling Glory around. But how could I know—"

"She's okay, right? And you're fine?"

"Sure, we were just spectators."

"Sarah's okay?"

"Oh, yeah. Novak's the one who was hurting."

"When we get through this, Vince, we've got to come up with another plan for Glory. We can't raise her this way."

"It's more educational than TV," I said, hoping for a smile.

"It's not normal," she countered.

"Who said normal's the best way?"

"I can't believe they're moving this fast on the construction," she said. "I don't think we can pull something together by tomorrow to stop them."

"That's probably the idea."

Our phone rang.

"Probably the SCALD hotline," I said. "Word's getting out."

Deb answered, listened a moment with a look of disgust, then handed me the phone. "It's Jack Reynolds."

"What does he want?" I mouthed.

She shrugged, then caught Glory midbounce and took her from the room.

"Jack, what can I do for you?"

"I just called to let you know that since the weather's clearing, the full-moon paddle is back on. We're meeting at Benoit Beach at nine-thirty."

"I can't make it, Jack. My kayak and gear are impounded at state police barracks. Don't ask. It's a long story."

"I suppose. Tell you what—I have an extra boat and gear I

can bring for you. Then you won't have to miss. It's going to be great out there tonight."

"It's going to be cold," I said.

"Nah. The wind's dying off. Don't be a wimp."

"I'll pass."

He wouldn't give up, so I changed tactics. "I have to stay home and watch Glory, Jack. Deb's got a SCALD meeting— they're arranging a picket line to meet your equipment to-morrow morning at Explorer's Park."

He was silent for a moment; then, rather than argue about the merits of development, as I'd expected, he again sug-gested the paddle would be fun.

An incoming call gave me a reason to cut him off. I switched lines. It was Sarah Dodge.

"I have some good news for Deb," she said. "I had to drive to the next county to find a judge, but SCALD got a tempo-rary injunction against the city. They can't start clearing the park tomorrow."

"Darn, I just had Jack Reynolds on the other line. If I'd known that, I'd have patched him in and let you tell him yourself."

"Speaking of Jack, Elaine and I'd like to meet you tonight if you're available. Can you swing by my office around eight?"

"Let me check with Deb. Now that she won't have to spend the night recruiting people to lie down in front of the dozers, I'm pretty sure she won't mind. But what does it have to do with Jack?"

"We'll tell you when you get here," she said.

Considering that she'd pulled off a minor miracle for SCALD this afternoon and Reggie Novak was back in jail, I expected Sarah to maybe crack a smile when I arrived. Instead she was all business.

"Come in," she said. "Elaine's back in the office."

I followed her past the reception area. Elaine was tucking a file into a drawer as we entered, and she greeted me with a shy, "Hello." She wore the same gray hoodie she'd had on last night but seemed less withdrawn inside it, probably the freedom she felt with her ex in jail.

"Okay, you've piqued my curiosity. Why'd you want to see me, and what does it have to do with Jack Reynolds?"

"We think he hired Reggie to steal the Sorenson journals," Sarah said.

I looked from one woman to the other, trying to gauge if they were pulling my leg, before I remembered that Sarah Dodge didn't have a sense of humor.

"Why would he?"

"I got to thinking about it on my drive back to Apostle Bay this afternoon," Sarah said. "That's when I realized that I hadn't actually listened to jerk-face this morning before I maced him. I'd assumed he was after Elaine, but when I thought back to the things he said, he seemed more interested in retrieving the judge's materials than finding her. In fact, it was when I told him that I gave the stuff to you so that you could publish the details in the newspaper that he flipped."

"You told him that? I didn't have the stuff for more than a few hours—thanks to you."

"Well, maybe I was goading him," she admitted.

"Great," I said, making sure she caught the sarcasm in my voice. "Okay, let's say Reggie did come here this morning in search of the judge's papers. What's the link to Jack?"

"Jack believes the judge found a way to stop, or at least significantly delay, the development," Sarah said. "He needed to destroy those documents."

"But the judge didn't," I said. "It was wishful thinking at best. Reynolds knew that."

"The judge was close," Elaine said in her quiet voice. "He'd been real excited the last few days before . . ."

"Here's the thing, Vince," Sarah said. "The judge *told* his nephew he had the proof. Elaine overheard them arguing the afternoon before the council meeting."

I looked to Elaine for confirmation, and she nodded.

"What did you hear?

"Peter was arguing with him again about money. He said the development sounded like a great idea and that they should invest in it, not fight it."

Sarah added, "Elaine says that's when the judge told Peter he was going to pay for SCALD's legal battle."

"They argued," said Elaine. "The judge said he'd found proof their family didn't even own the land."

I sighed and said, "It was just some vague passage in the journal, not proof."

"No, there was more," Elaine said. "It wasn't something in the journal. The proof was hidden elsewhere, and he thought he'd figured out where."

"Where?" I asked.

She looked at the floor. "I don't know."

"But he seemed sure?"

"Absolutely," Elaine said.

I thought about that a moment, then told them Monty's version of things.

"Even if the judge was bluffing, I still don't see how that involves Jack."

"Jack Reynolds and Peter Sorenson have been in bed

together on this," Sarah said. "Peter tells Jack; Jack hires Reggie. Destroy the proof before it's public, and the show goes on. If there is no real proof, well, no loss to Jack in that regard either."

"Yeah, but Jack and Reggie Novak don't hang in the same social circles."

"Reggie worked for him," Elaine said.

"He was a laborer for Jack before he went to jail," Sarah said.

"You know where this is heading," I said.

"Yes," Sarah said. "It means Reggie probably killed the judge. You may recall I said that from the get-go."

I checked Elaine's reaction. She wouldn't meet my eyes.

"I doubt even Jack would go to that extreme," I said.

"He didn't know that Reggie's a loose cannon," Sarah said. Elaine winced.

"I'll bet," Sarah continued, "that he's sweating right now with Reggie in jail, worried that he might talk."

I leaned back, considering her theory. "It sounds plausible," I said. "Good luck convincing the cops. Have you tried them yet?"

"Chief Weathers was gone when I returned to town," Sarah said. "I don't mind calling him at home, but I wanted to run it by someone else first. I'm not objective when it comes to Elaine's tormentor."

Her mentioning the chief reminded me about the GHB. I let them know it was used on the judge.

"That clinches it," Sarah said. "Guys like Reggie use that stuff."

I thought about that a moment, then pulled out my cell phone. "Jack Reynolds invited me out for a paddle tonight. "If he hasn't left yet, maybe I'll join him."

Chapter Forty-three

Jack's Hummer looked like an upside-down seaplane with the two kayaks on top. It was the only vehicle at the Benoit Beach parking lot when I arrived.

Reynolds stood down by the water's edge, facing the lake, one hand held to his ear, the other gesturing. Either he was talking on his cell or praying to the spirit of the lake. My money was on the cell.

Small waves shimmered out in the bay. They rolled ashore and disappeared like glitter on the sand. A half mile to my left, sodium vapor lamps cast an orange glow on the empty ore dock.

Jack turned my way when I closed the car door. He waved, ended the call, and strode up through the dune grass.

"Where's everyone else?" I asked when he reached the lot.

"It's just you and me," he said. "I was just checking messages to see if anyone else had a change of heart."

He wore shorts, a waterproof, long-sleeved paddling top,

and Tevas. A gentle but chilly breeze came onshore and had me rethinking the intelligence of this outing.

"The instructor's not coming?"

"Nah. I couldn't reach him to explain we were back on. Besides, it's a calm night, and we're not going far. You and I can handle it alone. Not worried, are you?"

I shrugged.

Jack chuckled, then said, "Good, give me a hand with these boats."

I helped him lift the kayaks down, and we carried them to the water's edge. Jack's kayak was a red and white fiberglass boat with sleek, straight lines and hard chines. He'd brought a red plastic, blow-molded boat for me that was similar to my own with a rounded bottom and wider cockpit.

We made another trip to gather paddles, spray skirts, and PFDs—personal flotation devices. I asked Jack if he had an extra wet suit.

"No need. Besides, they're too constricting."

Maybe for someone so full of himself, I thought.

"This will be a piece of cake," he added. "The lake's calm, we're not in a hurry, you won't even get wet—unless, of course, you want to practice your *C*-to-*C*."

"I plan to keep my head above water tonight," I said.

I stepped into the spray skirt, a neoprene corset designed to keep water from splashing into the cockpit. Then I donned the PFD, adjusting the straps to fit my smaller frame. I was stalling, debating if I should back out. This had sounded like a much better idea back at Sarah's office.

"C'mon," Jack said. I heard a touch of humor in his voice. "We're not going on a major excursion. You don't need all that gear."

He'd tucked his spray skirt behind his seat and his PFD

into the cargo cords crossing the front of his hull. Then he slid into his boat's narrow opening and, doing a monkey walk on his fists, pushed into the lake. He paddled a few strokes and then turned.

"Let's go, Vince."

"Yeah, give me a minute. I wanted to—"

Reynolds paddled away.

I leaned headfirst into my boat and adjusted the foot pegs to match my shorter frame, knowing the craft would be hard to balance if I couldn't brace my feet and thighs against the hull, and also hoping he'd return while I dinked around and then I could ask a few questions before getting onto the lake. I'd planned to pump Jack for information on the beach first, but he was already a hundred yards away and turning off-shore.

I climbed in and struggled to stretch the skirt over the cockpit's lip. Jack, meanwhile, continued paddling. By the time I'd shoved off, taken a few strokes, and tried to get a feel for the boat's stability, he'd turned a wide circle and glided back beside me.

"Let's head east toward the Silver River," he said, pointing in the opposite direction of the ore dock with his paddle. "We can get away from the dock's lights and enjoy this moon. Plus, it keeps the wind at our side. It's not often we get clear sky on a night like this."

I looked in the direction he pointed in, and although I knew there were houses near the shore, including the judge's, I couldn't see lights and decided it was too deserted for my comfort level.

"I'd rather explore around the ore dock. You know, take advantage of no boats being there."

Jack shrugged. "Sure. Whatever."

We paddled in that direction, Jack taking one stroke for every three of mine. I relaxed and tried thinking about my paddling for a moment, remembering to push the paddle through the recovery rather than pulling it back. As usual, it seemed awkward for me, and my arms felt tired by the time the ore dock loomed over us. We both stopped and drifted, looking up at the massive concrete columns and iron chutes folded against the beast's body like armored wings.

"So, you already have construction equipment at Explorer's Park," I said.

"What, no recorder?" Jack said. "No notebook or pen?"

"I have a great memory."

"Yeah, so you said. Public works has equipment onsite. It's not a secret. They'll start tomorrow despite any protest, finish clearing the park this fall, and construction will start in the spring."

"You think so?"

"I know so."

Jack paddled east, and we moved offshore toward the end of the structure.

"Then you haven't heard?"

"What? Your wife and Team Granola have a protest planned? Like I said, tell them not to waste their time. Life moves forward. It's called progress."

"SCALD got an injunction this afternoon. It's called the law."

"Right. Who heard the case? Dexter's ghost?"

"A circuit judge down in Hiawatha County."

He cursed, and the sound echoed off the structure. "Wait, you're pulling my chain, aren't you?"

"Nope."

"It won't hold," he said. "We've done everything by the book."

Reynolds plunged his paddle and pulled away from me. He rounded the far side of the structure. I let him go, figuring he could stew over that a moment before I tried my gambit on the journals.

I caught up with him on the far side, and we drifted through shadows cast by the massive structure. Small waves lapped against the pilings. Reynolds seemed relaxed again.

"Do you know how much ore comes down one of these chutes?" he said, pointing up with his paddle toward the metal pans seventy feet above us. I knew there were a hundred chutes on each side of the dock from a feature story I'd once written, and when an ore boat parked under them, railroad workers would crank the chutes down and aim them toward openings in the ship's deck.

"Two hundred and twenty tons of iron pellets," he said, "destined to become cars and trucks and metal roofs, Vince. Things you and I and everyone else use every day. And it's here because Randolph Sorenson had a vision and the courage to pursue it. That's what this town needs right now. Vision. Tax revenue is stagnant. We've cut city services. Without growth Apostle Bay will die. We won't have the population to support the schools, we won't have—"

"Give it a rest, Jack. I've heard it before."

"But have you listened?"

"Funny, you mentioned Randolph Sorenson," I said. "I heard you were in the market for his journals."

Reynolds chuckled. He turned his boat 180 degrees with a quick scull so we faced in opposite directions, me toward the ore dock, him away. "Where'd you hear that?"

"Does the name Reggie Novak ring a bell?" I asked.

Reynolds grabbed my boat's cargo bungee to hold us together. He stared at me, and I suspect he was debating whether to lie or not.

"I had the journals for a few hours last night," I said. "Interesting reading."

"What do you mean *had*?"

"I gave them to the police."

Reynolds pulled closer to me, until our cockpits were side by side. "You gave them everything?"

"Yeah, why?"

Jack let go of my boat, patted his pockets, and then reached forward and checked the pocket of his PFD. He grunted a curse.

"What's wrong?" I said. "I'm sure the chief will give you a look."

When Reynolds looked my way, I knew what was coming but couldn't react fast enough. He grabbed my arm. With a quick jerk he pulled me toward him and then down into the water. I almost saved it at the tipping point, but Jack got his other hand on my head and shoved me under.

The cold shock constricted my chest, forcing the air out of me. It was dark and wickedly cold, far colder than the pool. And my jacket, now wet, restricted me to slow motion.

I thrashed, shoving against the foot pegs and clawing the spray skirt. My lungs were going to explode.

Stop struggling, I told myself. Stay calm.

I ran my fingers around the neoprene's edge, trying to peel it loose, and my hand caught the release strap. I yanked and pushed against the pegs. The skirt pulled free, and I fell out.

Struggling to swim in my clothes, I found the surface and

tried to suck a mouthful of air. The cold was like a clamp on my chest.

I grabbed the inverted kayak and pulled myself halfway on top, then rested until I got enough oxygen to clear my head. My paddle floated nearby, and I grabbed it. I was shivering, but the fear had passed.

Reynolds was turning the corner of the ore dock, heading back the way we'd paddled.

"Jack, hey, come back! Jack!"

My mind worked on two levels. One walked me through the rescue drill that I'd done in the pool: flipping the boat, slipping the paddle into the cord that stretched from the kayak's front to back so I wouldn't lose it while maneuvering myself into the cockpit.

I'd only practiced rescues in the pool wearing a swimsuit. Fully clothed, I moved more slowly. Plus, the boat, being mostly full of water, wobbled more than usual. It wasn't going to sink, but cockpit's lip was inches above the surface.

On the second level, I replayed our conversation, trying to remember what had set Reynolds off. He'd seemed a little angry when I told him about the journals, but that shove came out of nowhere. What did he think—I wasn't going to make it back to the beach?

"You're dead meat when I get back!" I yelled, knowing he could hear me through the ore dock's pilings. My voice echoed off the concrete.

My hands already hurt, and I recalled that the instructor had said the body shunts blood away from the extremities to protect the core. The memory gave me a kick in the behind, and I pulled myself across the cockpit. The boat swayed and threatened to tip.

The wind had pushed me up against a concrete piling, and

I grabbed it, trying to propel the kayak toward shore. I was only a few hundred feet away, and even though the pilings were slimy and hard to grab, that seemed more efficient than taking a chance of capsizing again while trying to get back into the cockpit. The instructor had explained the importance of staying out of the water. Heat loss happened faster when you were immersed.

I worked my way closer to shore and, as I did, enjoyed fantasies of things I'd do when I caught up with Jack. I knew I wasn't in danger, just in for an uncomfortable walk back to my car.

I reached land and pulled myself onto the shore, stopping only a moment to catch my breath and peel off the PFD and skirt. I didn't bother with Jack's kayak. That thing could sink or get crushed by the next ore boat for all I cared.

Overhead, a railway trestle bridged the gap between the elevated rails that ran west of town and the ore dock. I stood on a rugged mound of granite that looked purple in the moonlight. A ten-foot security fence barred my way farther.

I debated climbing it as my eyes followed it down to the water and decided it would be easier to slip back into the water briefly and go around it. Had I attempted the climb, I'd most likely be found in the morning hanging by my ankles. The water's icy shock seemed a hair more tolerable this time around, and at least I was on my feet.

I pulled myself onto the slippery granite on the far side of the fence and climbed to the road. From here it was a half mile to the beach parking lot—a ten-minute jog in wet clothes, I figured. Maybe I could even beat Reynolds back.

Chapter Forty-four

I sprinted about a hundred yards, jogged another hundred, and then trudged the remainder, weighed down by saturated clothing and exhausted by my struggle in the water.

Partway back to Benoit Beach I heard approaching sirens. Past a clump of trees I saw red and blue flashers ahead at the parking lot.

I arrived at the lot at the same time the EMS wagon did. An Apostle Bay patrol car, white with blue and red markings, blocked Jack's Hummer. I recognized the chief's sedan behind the patrol car and saw a group of people between the Hummer and Deb's car. Radios crackled, and spotlights crisscrossed the lake.

I held back, trying to figure out what was going on.

"Where is he?" someone shouted. It sounded like Freeman, and it came from a figure holding another man in a half nelson, pressed against the Hummer's passenger door.

"Get this buffoon off me, Weathers." Definitely Reynolds'

voice, although it sounded as if the words were forced out one side of his mouth.

"Where's Vince?" the chief said. He stood near the two men and leaned one arm against the vehicle.

I approached, keeping on the far side of the patrol car.

"I've already told you," Reynolds said. "The last I saw, he was paddling around the ore dock."

"That's a lie!" I shouted. I started around the patrol car, building to a run, shouting something else unintelligent, and launched myself at Reynolds. Time seemed to move in slow motion then: me shouting at Reynolds; Freeman's and the chief's eyes widening in recognition; my arm cocking back for a roundhouse blow to the side of Reynolds' head as Freeman held him crushed against the Hummer's safety glass; the chief intercepting me, ducking under my wild swing, and lifting me off the ground; my face twisting slowly sideways to bounce off the back of the chief's hard head, sending a bolt of white light behind my eyes.

Time returned to normal speed as he set me down where I'd stood moments earlier.

"Whoa, Vince," he said. "Where'd you come from?"

"That jerk flipped my boat," I said between gulps of air. "I made it ashore at the ore dock and walked back."

"He's full of—" Reynolds shouted, but he couldn't finish because Freeman, who'd eased his pressure when I came at them, now mashed Reynolds' face into the glass, cutting off the words. For the first time since I'd known Freeman, I was glad for the detective's overkill. I also noticed the chief didn't tell him to back off and thought that an interesting sign.

"Are you okay, Vince?" the chief asked, holding me back and studying me.

I nodded, but at that moment my legs turned to jelly, and I

collapsed against the chief. The EMTs must have approached, because someone else grabbed me under one arm, and with the chief they walked me to the rescue vehicle.

"I'm fine," I mumbled.

The EMTs wrapped me in a blanket.

"Are you sure?"

"Don't believe Jack," I said.

"Take care of him," the chief told the EMTs. "I have to call off the search."

"Search?" I asked.

"All I asked for was a few days, Vince. Couldn't you even give me that?"

The EMTs gave me a once-over and determined I was nothing more than wet and cold. Once they'd peeled off my clothes and helped me into some spare scrubs, I started to be a little more coherent. After I stopped shivering and had a brief argument with the chief, they even let me drive to city hall, where the cop shop was buzzing as if it was the day shift.

A patrol officer let me in the back security door, telling me the media was out front, not realizing I was the media. Deb was waiting for me in the chief's spartan office, hair pulled up in a ponytail and tucked through the back of a ball cap.

I still had no idea why the cops had been at the beach but got an inkling when Deb flew out of her chair and met me with a hug, then a scowl.

"Are you out of your mind?" she shouted.

"Huh?"

She pushed away, putting some distance between us. "This is nuts. I thought you'd grown up since last year, but things haven't changed."

"What?" I said. "What do you mean?"

"What I mean," she said, jabbing a finger in my direction, "is why, when I'm sitting quietly at the kitchen table grading papers, do the cops show up and tell me that a maniac wife-beater is outside stalking our house—"

"Huh?"

"—while you're paddling a kayak out on the world's largest lake, in the middle of the night, alone with a killer, and they've called the Coast Guard to come rescue you—"

"Deb, hold on—"

"Our daughter's been kidnapped, you've been assaulted, a murder weapon's been found in your car, and I've been threatened with a lawsuit, and that's only in the last month." The tears were coming now, a rare sight on my supremely self-confident wife. Her lips quivered as she rushed to finish. "Did I leave anything out?"

"Back up a minute," I said, stepping toward her, wanting to pull her into a hug, but she stiff-armed me. "Someone tried to break into our house? What—"

"If you'd been home, you'd know," she said, and she turned away, facing the wall.

I felt stupid, not sure whether I should go to her or give her space. And still not clear on what had happened.

I heard a cough behind me and turned to see Gord at the door.

"Want a few more minutes?" he asked.

I looked toward Deb, but she didn't respond.

"No. Maybe you can enlighten me. It seems I'm out of the loop."

Gord started to say something, probably to chastise me; then I saw he reconsidered.

"Here's what we've pieced together," he said. "Maybe you can fill in some of the blanks."

"Sure."

"Sarah Dodge called me sometime after she spoke with you earlier this evening. She'd tried the chief first, but he wasn't home. She unloaded her theory on me, unaware that this afternoon Jack Reynolds paid Reggie Novak's bail."

"What?"

"Yep. Sarah flipped when I told her. Then she explained that you'd gone off on your idiotic attempt to play detective with Jack. She also explained that she'd led Reggie to believe you had the judge's documents. She's feeling a little bit responsible right now because she set all this into motion, unintentionally, but . . . Anyway, Sarah figured Jack's invite to you was a ploy to get you away from the house so Reggie could break in and search for the documents. He'd probably counted on Deb's being at the SCALD protest meeting, since I believe you told him there was one."

"What about—"

"Let me finish," Gord said. "I paged the chief—"

"He was with my mother, no doubt."

"—and then met a patrol car at your house, where we found Reggie. He was scoping out your place. We gave him a free pass back to the county lockup. The chief was worried about what Jack might be planning, especially since you'd put yourself in a bad position, so he called in reinforcements."

"The Coast Guard?" I asked.

"And the fire department. Archie got to the beach first, just as Jack was pulling in with his kayak." Gord chuckled. "I guess he welcomed him in typical Freeman fashion."

"I saw and will cherish that moment for quite a while."

Gord turned serious again. "I'll tell you, Vince, you gave the chief a scare. When he arrived, and Reynolds was there without you, the boys tell me he got scary."

Deb had apparently turned around and said, "He wasn't the only one worried. How do you think I felt when I learned you were out there with a killer?"

"We don't think he's a killer," Gord said.

"Stop defending him," Deb said.

"I wasn't in danger, Deb. He never once threatened me. Besides, I can take care of myself."

Deb snorted. "You can take care of yourself? Oh, get real. You've needed the ambulance twice in two days. You're a walking trauma patient."

"I wasn't in danger," I repeated. "In fact, now that I know about Reggie, it all makes sense. Jack flipped me after I told him I gave the journals to the cops. He must have been trying to delay me while he got back to his cell phone and called off Reggie."

I turned toward Gord. "You're still going to arrest him, though, right?"

Gord suddenly felt the need to inspect the linoleum.

"It's one thing to risk your own life," Deb said, now coming across the room and poking me in the chest. "It's another to put Glory and me in danger."

"But how could I have known—"

"Exactly," the chief growled behind me. He walked past us and sat down behind his desk. Then he waved us toward the visitor chairs. I dropped into mine, avoiding Deb's eyes. She slumped too. Gord moved over to lean one arm on the chief's gray file cabinet.

"For once you got it right, Vince," the chief said with that I'm-so-disappointed-in-you tone that made me feel as if I was in the principal's office back in second grade. "You couldn't have known because you don't have all the information. That is exactly why you keep endangering yourself and your family and, to be frank, screwing things up for us. Despite what you might think, we are actually capable of doing our job. I told you to stay home for a few days and let me handle it. Why is that such a difficult thing?"

"But, Chief—"

"It was a rhetorical question. Here's another one. Have you ever thought how much more efficiently we'd be able to do our job if we spent all our time enforcing the law and investigating crime instead of running off to rescue you every other day?"

"But, Chief—"

"I'm going to tell you where we are, not because it's any of your business, or because I want it to show up in tomorrow's *Chronicle*. I'm going to tell you so you'll see we do have a plan and you can go back to what you're supposed to be doing, which, if I understand correctly, is being a father. By the way, the one weakness your father admitted to me on several occasions, including on his deathbed, was that he regretted neglecting you and getting so emotionally wrapped up in his work. Don't make the same mistake."

I glanced over at Deb. She was still looking at her hands. Gord was now inspecting the ceiling.

"We've suspected Reggie Novak of killing the judge for some time," the chief said. "And we've been building a case—in spite of you. But now you've forced our hand, and we'll have to charge him tomorrow."

"And Jack Reynolds?" Deb asked.

"Jack's been released. We have no evidence of any connection between Reynolds and Novak beyond the bail. Jack says he was just helping out a former employee. Reggie isn't talking."

"Chief, that's a load of—"

"Vince, what did I just say? Let us do our job. One step at a time. The investigation is ongoing."

"But what about tonight?" I said.

"Yes," Deb added. "Surely Jack implicated himself."

"How? Jack Reynolds tells us that you contacted him and arranged the trip. Did you call him and set it up?"

"Not exactly. He—"

"He claims you pumped him for information. In fact, he says the entire trip was a ploy by you to get an interview. Based on what Sarah Dodge told Detective Greenleaf, I'd say there was some small amount of truth to that."

"He pushed me into the lake!"

"You do have a habit of annoying people when you're in reporter mode."

"This is absurd," I said.

"I agree," the chief answered. "If you'd done what I asked, we wouldn't be having this conversation."

Chapter Forty-five

We got out of city hall after midnight. Glory was asleep at Mom's house, and since she was going to be there the next day anyway, Mom ordered us to leave her. Deb and I agreed we were both too tired for another confrontation—we'd deal with it tomorrow.

I didn't sleep well and didn't bother trying after 5:00 A.M. Instead, I went to the office, where I found Lou brewing the morning's pot. He was clean-shaven, wore wrinkle-free clothes, and seemed less cantankerous than he'd been the past few weeks. I wondered at the change.

"John Reigle kicked me out of downstairs," he explained. "He even volunteered to take a pay cut if I'd just leave things to him. I gave him a raise. He deserves double his pay for the way he keeps that press working, but I can't afford that. Anyway, being down on my hands and knees so often was killing me. So, what have you got for me today?"

"How about a column explaining what a jerk Jack Reynolds

231

is?" I said. "Last night he hired a murderer to rob my house, and he tried to drown me."

"I see." Lou sipped from one of his coffee mugs and studied me. "And there's a police report stating that?"

"Not exactly."

"I'm afraid our readers are losing interest in your antics."

"Sheesh, me too," said Gina Holt as she came into the newsroom. She dropped her purse and coat onto her desk and then went to the fax machine to grab the overnight news releases. She swung by me and slapped the stack against my chest. "Doormat."

"Huh?"

"You heard me," she said.

"SCALD got an injunction to stop the Explorer's Park development," I said. "You might want to have Mort look into it."

"Or Ashley," Lou said. "It ties in with her story about Peter Sorenson's investing in the project."

"Yeow. Has the dirt even settled on the judge's grave?" I asked.

"Look at this," Gina said, waving a fax. "Rudy Clark has a news conference at ten this morning."

"Another announcement about his candidacy?" I asked.

"They've arrested someone in the judge's death."

"Should've known he'd take credit for that," I said.

"You knew?" Lou asked.

"I just told you. Jack Reynolds hired a murderer to rob my house."

"Did you plan to share that with us anytime soon?" he asked.

"It all went down last night. I was going to tell Ashley when she came in this morning."

He shot me a skeptical look.

"Really," I said. "The cops have been building a case against a guy named Reggie Novak. He's the psycho they arrested at Sarah's law office yesterday, the one who threatened the judge. I told you then it was probably related to the judge's death."

"Call Ashley at home and give her a heads-up. Ten's cutting it too close for us; she'll need the story written before the prosecutor's announcement."

"Doormat," Gina mumbled.

I grabbed a cup of joe, then called Ashley's cell and left her a message.

Ashley blew past my desk in her Capri pants and three-quarter–length top at ten to seven and parked herself by Lou.

"I just got off the phone with Rudy Clark," she announced. "He authorized a charge of open murder, against some guy named Reggie Novak. The arraignment's at nine, followed by his news conference. Clark gave me the details so I could make deadline instead of going to the conference."

"Unbelievable," Mort Maki said. "Clark has never helped us meet deadline."

"He's never campaigned for judge before either," I said. "This is free advertising."

"Write the story," Lou said. "But we'll hold it until after the arraignment. You go; Vince'll stay on the desk and wait for your call with any changes. And bring the photographer."

Gina coughed and shook her head.

When Ashley and our photographer left for the arraignment two hours later, I opened the shared network folder and pulled up Ashley's story.

JUDGE'S DEATH RULED MURDER: EX-CON ARRESTED

APOSTLE BAY—Police have arrested Apostle Bay resident Reginald Novak for the murder of Superior County Circuit Court Judge Dexter Sorenson. Sorenson was found four days ago, hanged from a tree in Explorer's Park.

Novak, 32, a three-time domestic violence offender, allegedly made good on his courtroom threat made two years ago that he would kill the judge when released from jail, said county prosecutor Rudy Clark.

"We arrested Novak without incident last night after conducting a thorough investigation," Clark said this morning.

Evidence against Novak, presented by detectives from the Apostle Bay police department at the arraignment this morning, includes footprints found at the judge's house the night of his death, a witness who saw Novak's vehicle at the judge's house, and physical evidence including fibers and fingerprints that place the suspect inside the judge's home the night of the alleged murder.

Clark also revealed at this morning's hearing that an autopsy showed that Judge Sorenson was drugged before being hanged. A compound commonly referred to as Liquid Ecstasy, or GHB, was found in the judge's blood. Novak has been linked to GHB. . . .

Ashley also mentioned that Novak was a suspect in a local assault and robbery. She finished the article with a quote from the judge's nephew.

Peter Sorenson, the judge's nephew and heir, said he was pleased to hear of the arrest.

"I can rest easier now, knowing that my uncle didn't commit suicide," he said. "I never believed that he had, but knowing for sure is a relief and a blessing."

Said Clark, who is currently running a write-in campaign to replace the judge, "I'm pleased to be . . .

"Gag me," I said to no one in particular. "Lou'll whack that last sentence."

"I hear you," Gina said.

"You reading Ashley's story too?"

"Yeah. Notice anything interesting in it?"

"That Clark seems to be her best friend?"

"Not what I meant," she said.

"Then what—"

My phone interrupted us, and I picked it up to hear Ashley's voice.

"Just got out of the hearing," Ashley said. "I have a few minor changes."

"Fire away, Ashley."

Gina shook her head and turned back to her work.

Chapter Forty-six

For the next several days I think I met everyone's expectations, except Lou's: I cared for Glory, mostly at our home; I left the police alone; and I stayed out of the local news.

I'd had two days off work, and local happenings were quiet enough that Lou didn't call. I found myself checking my voice mail even though I hadn't missed any calls.

When I did return to work—for instance, this morning— Lou gave assignments to Ashley and Mort and asked me to fill in with briefs. Gina seemed too busy with obits and community announcements to throw much harassment my way.

Indeed, I'd been so bored on the desk this morning that I'd called Greenleaf and talked him into meeting me at the Laughing Whitefish for lunch. I needed some kind of gossip fix.

I arrived early and snagged a booth in the corner farthest from the door. Greenleaf popped in soon after and shook his head when he saw me.

"What's wrong with our usual seats at the counter?" he asked.

"Nothing. I thought a booth would be a nice change."

"Uh-huh," he said, sliding in opposite me. "And I actually thought you invited me for my company."

"What? Can't we enjoy a little privacy for once?"

Gord rolled his eyes and picked up the menu.

"Maybe I did want to bounce an idea off you," I said.

"I knew it."

"I'm thinking about making a change."

"Going back to work full-time?"

"The opposite—I'm thinking about ditching the paper altogether and trying something else. They don't need me anymore. I feel kind of like a charity case there."

"What you really mean is that you can't stand not being the lead guy. Am I right?"

"No."

"Vince . . ."

"Okay, maybe. What do you think about my opening a day care place at our house? You know, just a few kids along with Glory."

"Are you out of your mind?"

"What?"

Gord chuckled. "Please, Vince, for my sake, come up with a different plan."

"I think it's a great plan."

"What did you do yesterday?"

"Spent the day with Glory."

"Doing what?"

"Coloring, reading books, going to the park. It was fun."

"Did you bring your cell?"

"Yeah, in case we had an emergency."

"Did you check your e-mail while you were coloring?"

"Only a few times."

"Right," he said, knowing the truth even if I wouldn't admit it. "What's Deb think of this idea?"

"I haven't run it by her yet."

Greenleaf shook his head. The waitress came, and we ordered. He picked his standard Reuben; I went for the soup of the day. When the waitress left, I changed the subject.

"There's one thing I can't let go about the judge, Gordon."

"Only one thing?"

"Yeah. Was he bluffing about being able to stop the Explorer's Park development? I've just been thinking—purely for selfish reasons, I admit—how great it would be if he had found a way to stop the development. Jack Reynolds deserves that."

Gord sipped his water and studied me. "Based on his notes, the judge wasn't bluffing," he said. "But whether there really is something is another story. Talk to Patrice about it. It makes more sense to her."

"Okay, I will. You haven't found a way to link Reggie and Jack, have you?"

"No. It's not going to happen either. Jack's too good."

"That stinks."

Gord sipped his water again and looked out the window toward the ore dock, where I'd been involuntarily swimming a few nights ago. "What do you think about Reggie Novak?" he asked.

"Why do you ask? Having second thoughts?"

"You know me. I like things tidy, no loopholes."

The cafe's door jangled, and I looked up to see Lucy DeMott enter, followed by Gina. Gina winked at me and then followed Lucy to the opposite end of the restaurant.

"What loopholes?" I asked.

"Between us?" he asked.

"Sure."

"The porn still bothers me. Remember I told you, it was clean. No fingerprints."

"Yeah, and the judge didn't have a DVD player."

"Well, Reggie seemed surprised about the porn, kind of like he was glad to hear that the judge wasn't so perfect. Not the response I'd expect if he'd planted it."

Greenleaf took another swallow of water. "Your car's another thing that bothers me," he said.

"I thought you guys found evidence that Reggie was inside it."

"Oh, he stole your car. I'm sure of that. It's the GHB we found that puzzles me. The bottle was clean. Why'd he wipe his fingerprints from that but not from the steering wheel or door handle? It doesn't make sense."

"Maybe he had to take off in a hurry and didn't get a chance."

"Maybe. But you know what? He's all but admitted to stealing your car, but when I asked about the drug, he seemed clueless. I just don't think he's that good of an actor."

"Sarah said he'd know about GHB."

"Sarah's a tad biased."

"You think?"

"The oil stains bother me too," Greenleaf said. "We found oil at the judge's house, in the street where we found your car after Reggie stole it, and in the street in front of Sarah's office."

"So?"

"We didn't find a trace in Explorer's Park."

"But there were new wood chips; maybe they got kicked around too much."

"No, we would have found it even on those chips. His truck wasn't there. So how'd he get the judge to the park?"

The waitress delivered our lunches. We both leaned back while she set the plates on the table and waited until she was out of earshot again.

"You're saying someone else helped Reggie."

Greenleaf shrugged and grabbed his sandwich.

"That would explain some of it," I said, trying to read him. "Probably the partner was smarter, more careful. Wore gloves when Reggie didn't. Maybe someone like Jack Reynolds?"

Greenleaf shook his head no. "Airtight alibi, remember?"

"What's his connection to Novak, then? Why pay the bail?"

"I think Reynolds creatively influenced Novak. I think he explained how important it was to make the judge's papers disappear, that sort of thing. He's too clever to give Novak a direct order; instead, he just suggested things. And I think Jack didn't realize that Novak was out of control. He bailed him out the first time to keep him quiet. He's abandoned him now."

"If not Reynolds, who? Another accomplice?"

Greenleaf shrugged.

"You have someone in mind, don't you?"

Greenleaf shrugged again, but I could tell he was getting uncomfortable, as if he'd said too much.

"Who? C'mon, buddy. Give me a hint at least."

"I'm not really sure what to think, Vince. I just don't want to look stupid on the witness stand. If I'm wondering these things, you know Novak's lawyer is going to wonder them too."

Chapter Forty-seven

Gord changed the subject, and we finished lunch, discussing the steelhead run and his analysis of Bay High's mediocre football season. He was a diehard alum and one of the school's few athletes who'd shown real talent.

Afterward Greenleaf insisted, as usual, on paying his own tab when we went to the counter. As we turned to leave, Gina called me over.

"Join us for a few minutes, Vince," she said, sliding over to the window side of her booth.

I told Greenleaf I'd see him around and stepped over to their table. Lucy wore jeans and a turquoise sweater.

"I didn't know you two were friends," I said.

"We're not," Gina said. I could tell she was itching for a smoke but couldn't inside the restaurant.

"We have a common interest," Lucy said.

I looked from one to the other; they were clearly dying to spill something but wanted to make me work for it.

"C'mon," I said. "Out with it."

241

"You know how Ashley's been kicking your butt?" Gina said.

"She hasn't been—"

"Yes, she has. It's pathetic."

"She's been kicking mine too," Lucy admitted.

"Don't tell me, you're starting a club of Ashley haters. Well, count me out. I've been thinking about quitting the *Chronicle* anyway."

"Talk about juvenile," said Gina.

"We were going to dish," Lucy said. "But if you're quitting, what's the point?"

I didn't move.

"Didn't think so," Gina said.

"Guess who your ace reporter is sleeping with," Lucy said.

"Huh?"

"You are so out of it, Vince," Gina said. "Peter Sorenson. She's dating the guy."

"Get out," I said.

"How did you think she was getting all those good quotes from him?" Lucy asked. "How does she get info about Sorenson and the estate one step ahead of everyone else? How'd she get details about the will?"

Gina and Lucy shared a laugh at this.

"What makes you think they're, you know . . . ?"

"We spied on them," Gina said.

"What?"

"She really ticked me off," Lucy said, as if that explained everything.

"Jeez, you haven't ever spied on me, have you?"

Lucy grinned, "You'll never find out—unless, of course, you yank the microphone away from someone I'm interviewing, which you won't have a chance to do after next week. I'm finally outta here."

"Contract is up?"

"Yep," she said. "I'm off to the NBC affiliate in Milwaukee."

"Good for you," I said. "You're pulling my leg, aren't you? About the spying, I mean?"

"Ya think so?" Gina asked.

"He spends most nights at her house," Lucy said.

"We think they haven't moved into the judge's place yet because he can't get rid of the housekeeper," Gina said.

Lucy lowered her voice. "I've got a neighbor watching them. She calls my cell every time they leave or arrive at Ashley's apartment."

"What?" I said, too loudly. Conversation stopped at the surrounding tables, and people stared at us. Gina and Lucy chuckled again.

"An old biddy," Gina said quietly. "She saw Lucy sitting out front one day and recognized her."

"I told her it was an undercover job," Lucy said. "I've been collecting footage of them together. I'm running the story tonight."

"No, you're not," I said.

"Sure am, and you know you're going to enjoy seeing it. Tune in at six."

I smiled at the thought. "How long has this been going on?"

Lucy shrugged. "Our source doesn't have the best of memories. At least a week, but we're not sure."

"It's good gossip, but it's not good news," I said. "They're consenting adults. If she wants to work that way, that's her prerogative."

"You are so full of it," Gina said.

"What if he's been influencing her stories?" Lucy asked.

"How?"

"Subtle ways. Like his being the heir to Sorenson's fortune."

"There's a will," I said. "It's pretty cut-and-dried."

"Then you haven't done your homework," Lucy said.

"I told you you've lost your edge," Gina said. "You probably should quit. In your prime you'd have been all over this."

I looked from one to the other but had no clue to what was up.

"Got any sources in probate?" Lucy asked.

I slapped my forehead. "There's a problem with the will?"

"Give that boy an *A* for finally using those gray cells," Gina said.

This must be what Gord had alluded to, I thought. Peter Sorenson was the accomplice. It fit. If he knew the judge was already dead, he could have been the person who tipped Ashley about the judge's body. That's why she was at Explorer's Park, and that's how she got all the background details by deadline. And he had the opportunity to plant the porn. It all made sense, if he was the heir. But—"

"Wait a minute. Are you telling me he's not the heir?"

"I'm not giving you everything," Lucy said. "In fact, I get the feeling I've given you a bigger jump start than I meant to."

"Tsk-tsk," said Gina. "This competition thing is rearing its ugly head again. Let's keep our eye on the target."

We both looked at her.

"Lucy's leaving town. Vince, you're either quitting or coming back to work. Either way, Lucy's running the story tonight, and you've got to follow up for Lou tomorrow—Ashley sure can't. She might not even have a job. How about a little more cooperation here? Lucy, tell Vince what you know."

"What's he have to offer?" Lucy said. "So far, it's been one-sided."

"I've been helping you," Gina said.

A thought crossed my mind, and I pulled out my cell phone. "Give me a minute," I said, and I dialed Gordon, probably catching him on his way back to the station.

"Hey, Gord, a question."

"I don't like that tone," he said. "Don't tell me I've gone and cranked you up again."

"A while back you told me you'd pulled Ashley's phone records to find out if she had a tip about the judge. What did you find?"

"Why do you ask?"

"Just a thought. C'mon, Gordon, I could get it with FOIA if I was writing a story, but I'm not. Who called her?"

There was a pause, and then he said, "Nobody. The best we can tell, her story was true—she happened across the judge while walking in the park."

"Nobody?"

"The first call she had that morning was an outgoing on her cell, and that would have been after Freeman was on the scene."

"Oh," I said.

"You sound surprised."

"Guess I am. I thought for sure she'd had a call. Thanks. Thanks for your time."

I closed the phone and looked from Gina to Lucy.

"What did he say?" Lucy asked.

"I was sure, from what you've just told me, that Peter was

involved in the judge's murder somehow and that he'd tipped Ashley. But Gord says he didn't."

"Peter? In on the murder?" Lucy asked.

I made her swear she wouldn't mention Gordon and then told both women about our conversation.

"Put it all together, and it makes me think Peter's the accomplice. I think Gord's on to him."

"This is even better," Lucy said. "The *Chronicle*'s reporter is sleeping with a murderer."

"Right. So tell me, what am I going to find at the probate court?"

"The judge's real will," Lucy said. "And Peter Sorenson is not the heir."

Chapter Forty-eight

I left the Laughing Whitefish Cafe reenergized. Not that I wanted to see Ashley burned for making a stupid mistake. Well, maybe I did want to see that. She should have known better.

I checked my watch and saw I had a half hour before picking up Glory at Mom's and taking her to this week's tea social. I drove to the historical society and parked near my usual spot in the back alley.

"Vince," Patrice said. "I wondered when you'd stop by. Usually you're so impatient for answers that you hound me. This time I thought I'd have to call you."

"I've been distracted. But it's time to finish what I started. Gordon told me you've had a chance to do your thing with the judge's notes and the journals."

"I've had a chance to look at them, if that's what you mean. They're a fascinating piece of this region's history."

"I know."

"Even if they have been mishandled," she added, looking at me in a way that made me swear I must have left grape Pop-Tart smears on the pages.

"Was the judge bluffing when he said he could stop the development?"

"I'd say from his notes that he was."

"Bummer. I was hoping you had better news."

"Bluffing, based on an educated guess and clever thinking."

"What's that supposed to mean?"

"To explain, I'd have to go—"

"Time's short. I need the edited version."

She gave me an exasperated look. "Always in a hurry, aren't you?"

I gave her what I hoped was a pitiful smile.

"Okay, I didn't catch anything of substance until I read the judge's notes, and then Monty Haver stopped by—I guess I have you to thank for that. That's when I realized what the judge was on to."

"And that was?"

"It seems the story got twisted over time in a critical way. Haver's family thought their forebear, Melvin Haver, hid the documents that prove his innocence—or Randolph Sorenson's guilt—at the general store. The judge thinks—excuse me, *thought*—it was really the post office where he hid them."

"But they were one and the same."

"Possibly. However, Melvin Haver, you may recall, was the postmaster for two post offices, Apostle Bay and—"

"And New Cumberland, the first settlement in the area up on the Silver River."

"Amazing. You actually retained some facts."

"Thanks. But I thought the New Cumberland facilities were destroyed in a flood."

"Most were, but you can still see the forge and a couple of stone walls. It's not much, but remember, the flood happened before Melvin Haver's death, so what's there now was also there during his time, albeit worse for the wear now."

"Yeah, except it didn't do his wife and family any good if they didn't know."

"It's only speculation, but I think they did know."

"Then why—?"

"Because in 1856, Vince, there was nothing a single mother could do, even with the proof. She was more concerned with her children's safety than her husband's reputation. Think about it: her husband questioned the town's leader, and he ended up dead and considered by most to be a thief. I think she knew, and she passed the info down from generation to generation, hoping that when the day was right, someone would bring it forward. The problem was, the information got misconstrued."

"Have you—"

"Told Monty? No. Not yet."

"Have you gone out to look? At the site?"

"Not yet. It's kind of complicated."

"Why?"

"I'm not sure who would own the documents, if, indeed, they are found. I want to clear that up first."

"Unbelievable," I said, wondering if there was any way I could get out to the site before I needed to pick up Glory but knowing at the same time there wasn't. I needed to get over to Mom's pretty quickly as it was. "The fate of Explorer's Park is riding on this, you know."

"I wouldn't get too excited about saving Explorer's Park, because, as I said, this is all speculative."

"Yeah. Well, thanks, Patrice. I have to run."

She seemed surprised I was leaving.

"I need to pick up my daughter and get her somewhere."

"Oh. I thought you'd come to check on that other matter you asked me about—you know, whether I had any MSU colleagues who knew your new reporter, Ashley Adams?"

"Ugh," I said, slapping my forehead. "I completely forgot. What did you learn?"

She smiled, teasing. "Well, if you've got to go . . ."

"C'mon, what is it?"

"My colleagues said she was an aggressive student who made good grades and was considered a teacher's pet."

"That's it?"

"I also researched the MSU news archives to see some of the stories she'd written."

I wanted to kick myself. I should have thought of that. Gina was right about my losing it.

"I found an interesting piece she wrote about a chemistry student who was kicked out of school. He'd been caught manufacturing some kind of date-rape drug in the lab. You'll never guess who the student was."

"Actually, Patrice, I bet I can."

Chapter Forty-nine

Outside the historical museum I had to steady my hand to call Lucy DeMott.

"Lucy, it's Vince. Listen, you haven't told anyone else about your story yet, have you?"

"I was just getting ready to run it by our producer."

"Don't."

"What do you mean, don't?"

"I don't have time to explain right now, but please trust me. I'm going to give you a story that will end your time in Apostle Bay with a *huge* bang. Can you get to Lakeview Elder Care in a half hour?"

"That's cutting it close for me to edit."

"When you hear what I have, you'll agree it's worth it. Bring your film of Ashley and Peter. We'll need that."

"But what's this—"

"Lakeview in thirty minutes," I said, and I hung up. I walked around the building toward the alley where I'd parked and dialed the *Chronicle* next.

251

"Gina," I said. "Huge favor."

"I believe I already did you one this afternoon."

"You're right. I need another, and I know this will be nothing short of a miracle, but you've got to pull it off. It'll be way worth it. Get Lou over to Lakeview Elder Care in the next fifteen minutes."

"Cripes, you don't ask for much. How am I supposed to pull that off?"

"You're creative. And, Gina, if Ashley's around, don't let her know what you're doing."

I hung up and made one more call. "Gord, you've got it wrong."

"Huh?"

"I can't talk now. Meet me at Lakeview Elder Care in fifteen minutes. Drop whatever you've got. And bring the chief too."

"Vince, I thought . . ."

I flipped the phone shut and climbed into the Bronco. If I hurried, I'd even have Glory to tea on time.

Chapter Fifty

I was so jittery the next morning at the *Chronicle,* I was afraid to drink coffee. Once we'd convinced Lou to play along—and he didn't have much choice, because it was the only way Lucy DeMott agreed to hold her story—the plan came together well. Now I just hoped we could pull it off. Otherwise my decision to change careers would be made for me.

The chief had been equally hard to convince and even threatened to confiscate Lucy's tapes. She was too much of a veteran to fall for his bluff, and the chief knew if her story ran—well, it would make his job far more difficult.

Gina came in humming and wearing a huge grin five minutes after I did. I saw that the photographer, who normally wouldn't arrive for another hour, was already in. Lou must have briefed him.

At ten to seven Gina and I went to Lou's desk and set up. When Mort rolled in, we pulled him over. Ashley came in at seven.

She went to her desk, dropped her purse, and pulled out

her PDA. Then she seemed to notice us all around Lou's desk.

"What's going on?" she asked. "Big news?"

"Didn't you hear?" I said. "The prosecutor dropped the murder charge against Reggie Novak. They have a new suspect."

She looked puzzled. "What do you mean, they have a new suspect? Who?"

"Check out the story," I said, pointing to her monitor. "There's a copy in the shared folder. I wanted to get your feedback on it anyway."

"Lou," she said, "what's up? I thought—"

"It's breaking news, Ashley," he grumbled. "Happening as we speak."

She sat in her chair and reached for her mouse. I went to my desk and pulled up the story too, though I knew it by heart now.

APOSTLE BAY—Police arrested Apostle Bay Chronicle *reporter Ashley Adams and Peter Sorenson this morning for the alleged murder of Judge Dexter Sorenson. Peter Sorenson is the judge's nephew. . . .*

"What is this? Someone's idea of a bad joke?" Ashley said.

"No joke, Ashley," I said.

She studied me a moment, glanced back at her screen, and then stood.

"You know when I figured it out?" I said. "When I learned that you hadn't been tipped about the judge's body."

"I should've known you were behind this," she said.

"All along I'd thought you had a tip and that it was probably the killer who'd called you. Then Lucy DeMott showed me video she has of you and Peter—that was sloppy, letting her get film of you two together at your house. So I figured Peter was the killer, and that he tipped you off. I thought he was using you. Indeed, for a moment I actually felt sorry for you."

"What *are* you talking about?" she said, her voice calm. She folded her arms across her chest and leaned back. She was so relaxed, I had a moment of doubt.

"But the cops pulled your phone records, and there were no calls to you that morning. You hadn't been tipped."

"That's what I told everyone. It's not news."

"You didn't get a call because you already knew the judge was there."

"I was out for a walk."

"Big mistake, Ashley. You should have let someone else discover the body. But you couldn't let the story go, could you?"

"You're out of your mind," she said. Her smile grew smug.

"I've been kicking myself that I didn't make the Michigan State connection sooner. I should have figured it out when I saw Peter and his green and white Windbreaker the night of the vigil.

Ashley laughed. "That's weak. I'm guilty because we went to the same school?"

"No, because Peter was kicked out of school for manufacturing GHB in the chem lab, and you wrote the story about him."

"So what?" She turned toward Lou. "I didn't mention I knew Peter because I was afraid you'd pull me off the story. I wanted you to accept me as a journalist for my writing skills, not because of whom I knew."

"I stopped accepting you as a journalist when I saw the video last night, Ashley—the one that shows Peter going into your house at night and not coming until 8:00 A.M. the next day."

"That doesn't prove anything."

"It proves he was spending nights at your house," I said. "But you're right—that in itself doesn't prove you killed his uncle. However, your hair found on the judge's clothing has the cops wondering."

"My hair? You yourself saw me touch the body at Explorer's Park. A few strands of my hair on him don't prove a thing."

The chief walked into the room. "Except, Miss Adams, the hair was found underneath the judge's robes, not on the robes themselves. The only way it could have gotten there was if you'd helped dress him in the robes before hanging him."

"But that's—"

"Why'd you bother putting the robes on?" I asked. "Just to make it more dramatic? To get better art for your story?"

"I don't need this. I'm out of here," she said, grabbing her purse.

"Wait a minute," Maki said, and we all turned to look at him. "Is this true? They're executing a search warrant this morning at Ashley's house?"

I saw Ashley's face go pale.

"As we speak," the chief said. "Detective Greenleaf tells me that Peter Sorenson is already in custody and that he's talking."

"He'd never—" Ashley started, then cut herself off. She ran toward the door, and Freeman stepped in to block her escape. The photog started snapping photos.

"Oh, get real," she said, turning away from the camera.

"Have a seat," Freeman said.

Ashley turned in the other direction, and we could see her debating a run past the chief.

"What are they going to find at your house, Ashley?" I asked. "My money is on finding the new, fraudulent version of the judge's will on your computer. The judge didn't use computers, you know. He didn't type the new will Peter claimed to have discovered."

"Oh, shut up," she said.

"The porn was another mistake. Was that supposed to add drama too?

"Shut up!" she screamed.

A cell rang, and the chief flipped his open. He grunted, listened, and then said to us, "Greenleaf found GHB ingredients in her apartment."

"Has Peter perfected the mix?" I asked.

"I want a lawyer," Ashley said.

"We know you put the vial of it into my car," I said. "Were you just carrying it in your purse and saw the opportunity? Or were you trying to frame me?"

But Ashley had clamped her mouth shut. We weren't getting anything else out of her, I thought.

Lou watched her a moment, then turned to the photog. "Did you get some good art?"

The guy nodded, then stepped back into his lab.

"Good. Chief, if you don't mind clearing out of here, we've got a paper to put together," Lou said. Then he reached across his desk, grabbed one of his mugs, and sipped.

"Detective Freeman," the chief said. "Please give Miss Adams a ride to jail."

"Yeah, right," Ashley said. "What's he going to do, make me ride on his handlebars?"

I saw Freeman smile.

"I wanted to make you run behind," he said, grinning, and then he pulled a set of keys from his pocket and jangled them. "But I'm back in the saddle."

Chapter Fifty-one

Sunlight dappled through the trees, some of the first morning sun we'd seen in days, as we made our way up the Silver River hiking path toward the old Cumberland forge site. Crimson and yellow leaves swirled in the river's eddies, dancing with the water as it spilled over rocks and tumbled toward Superior.

Glory rode in the backpack, humming and kicking her legs to the rhythm of my steps. Behind us Deb and Gordon were chatting about birds. Gordon carried a shovel over one shoulder. Patrice led the way, surprising me in the way she darted up the path, her entire wiry self eager to reach the site.

I listened as Gordon filled in Deb on the case.

"Ashley broke first," he said. "She tried to pin everything on Peter, even implied he'd slipped GHB into her drink too, enough to influence her actions, which doesn't wash when you learn more of their history. Peter, of course, claims she masterminded the entire murder."

"Pathetic," Deb said.

"From what I can piece together, they started dating after she wrote the story about his expulsion from State. She was drawn to him because she thought he was wealthy."

"She used him too," Deb said.

"Peter came up last spring to get money from the judge for some venture, but his uncle sent him packing, and that's when he learned about the will—all Sorenson's wealth was slated to go into a foundation to be used for the community. The two of them came back after Ashley graduated. We're pretty sure the plan from the beginning was to kill the judge."

"Is Rudy Clark going for premeditation?" I asked over one shoulder.

"That's the hammer he's holding over their heads. Finding a credit card receipt in Ashley's apartment for a new rope bought at the hardware store seems to clinch it."

"At least until the election," I said.

Greenleaf let that pass.

"So they drugged the judge, hauled him to the park, and hanged him," Deb said. "Why not make it look like a simple robbery?"

"I'll bet it was Ashley's idea," I said. "It made a better story."

"Possible. Peter handed her the idea, though. He said his uncle had been going on and on about the historical hanging's probably being a murder, and he was sick of hearing about it."

"And you actually found the will on her computer?" I asked.

"It had been deleted but was still in the electronic trash. Better yet, we found scraps of paper where she'd practiced forging Judge Sorenson's name."

"If the estate goes into a trust, who controls it?"

"A committee of three," Greenleaf said. "The pastor of the judge's church, the Chamber of Commerce director, and Monty Haver."

We came around a bend in the river and into an area where the trees thinned. Patrice had stopped on the path about fifty yards ahead and waited for us.

Centered in the clearing, surrounded by brown grass and small trees, were the remains of an old furnace, the stones rising in the shape of a pyramid with a flattened top.

Parts of stone building foundations were visible around the clearing, and Patrice pointed out mounds buried under leaves, moss, and other material that had accumulated over the last century and a half.

Patrice compared a photocopy of an old map to the land itself and tried to figure out where the general store and post office would have been. I lowered Glory to the ground and let her run around the site while Patrice and Gordon counted paces and studied the map. They found the outline of a building. Most of the walls were crumbled and covered with vines and moss. A stone chimney stood at one wall, the broken mortar and rocks rising about eight feet.

"Keep a close eye on Glory," Gordon said. "There's poison ivy all over here."

Inside the general outline of the building it looked as if some kids, or maybe fishermen, had held a party. The grass was burned away, and blackened logs lay helter-skelter near a couple of faded beer cans. Someone had dragged in logs for seating.

"Broken glass too," Deb said.

"Back in the pack, little girl," I said.

I turned to grab Glory and saw she was at the chimney, pulling on the vines that covered it.

"Oh, no, Glory!"

Our daughter had a double handful of the stuff and looked up with excitement that changed to fear as both Deb and I ran toward her. Each of us took an arm and told her to drop the vine.

"Wipes," Deb said. "Get as much as possible wiped."

While Deb held her immobile, I stepped over to the backpack and grabbed the baby wipes. When I returned, Patrice was poking with a stick at the place where Glory had pulled away the poison ivy. She dug more frantically.

Deb and I meanwhile scrubbed Glory, hoping we could prevent the worst of the ivy's oil from spreading.

"Over here," Patrice said. "Bring me the shovel."

Gordon helped her.

"It's the old clean-out," he said.

Gord used the shovel to pull more of the ivy away. Meanwhile, I returned Glory to the backpack and lifted her onto my shoulders.

Gord used the shovel's point to pry the cast-iron door. Rather than open, the entire door and frame fell out with little resistance. Patrice looked at him, then squatted and looked into the hole. I tried to see over her but couldn't. It didn't matter, as moments later she stood up and turned to show us, cradled between two hands, wrapped in dried oilcloth, a stiff yellow pouch.

Epilogue

Most of the documents contained in the pouch Patrice found were decomposed to the point they were no longer readable, even after an expert she knew worked on them. But the most important document did survive, a deed proving Melvin Haver owned the land at the mouth of the Manitou River, received as a gift from Randolph Sorenson. Monty Haver negotiated an agreement with the city of Apostle Bay, allowing them to lease the land under the condition that it remain in its natural state. He added a memorial at the site honoring his great-great-grandfather.

Rudy Clark did not earn the most votes in November for the circuit court judge's race. That distinction went to the late Judge Dexter Sorenson, whose name had been printed on the ballot before his death. Clark tallied the second most votes and was sworn in as the new judge. I wanted to run the headline: *People Prefer Corpse to Clark*. Lou wouldn't let me.

Ashley Adams cut a deal and pleaded guilty to manslaughter in relation to the judge's death. She agreed to testify against Peter Sorenson in his trial, which has yet to be scheduled. He still faces a homicide charge and probably wishes he'd narced on Ashley first.

Reggie Novak was convicted of larceny, stalking, several counts of breaking-and-entering, and assault. He will spend most of his remaining life in jail. Kidnapping charges against him were dropped.

Lou has asked me to return to the newspaper full-time. I haven't decided whether I will but encouraged him to give Gina Holt a shot as a news reporter. I figure if, nothing else, she and the chief ought to get along like great pals.

Glory, it seems, is not susceptible to poison ivy. I, on the other hand, suffered dearly. The rash covered the entire back of my neck and head, places Glory so deftly patted while riding in the backpack.